ALICE IN ZOMBIELAND

ALICE IN ZOMBIELAND

LEWIS CARROLL AND NICKOLAS COOK

ILLUSTRATIONS BY SIR JOHN TENNIEL AND BRENT CARDILLO

sourcebooks

Published by Sourcebooks, Inc.
P.O. Box 4410, Naperville, Illinois 60567-4410
(630) 961-3900
Fax: (630) 961-2168
www.sourcebooks.com

Originally published in Winnipeg in 2009 by Coscom Entertainment.

Library of Congress Cataloging-in-Publication Data

Cook, Nickolas
  Alice in Zombieland / Lewis Carroll and Nickolas Cook ; illustrations by Sir
John Tenniel and Brent Cardillo.
    p. cm.
  Originally published: Winnipeg : Coscom Entertainment, 2009.
  1. Carroll, Lewis, 1832-1898. Alice's adventures in Wonderland. 2. Carroll,
Lewis, 1832-1898—Parodies, imitations, etc. 3. Zombies—Fiction. I.
Tenniel, John, Sir, 1820-1914. II. Cardillo, Brent. III. Title.
  PS3603.O57442A45 2011
  813'.6—dc22
                                    2010046785

Printed and bound in the United States of America.
VP 10 9 8 7 6 5 4 3 2 1

INTESTINES

CHAPTER I

DOWN THE DEAD-HOLE

ALICE was beginning to get very tired of sitting by her sister on the bank, and of having nothing to do. Her sister had seemed very displeased about having to accompany her against her will down to the graveyard that sprawled adjacent to their home. The graveyard, her favorite place to play, was all tangled gray vines and tilting ancient tombstones, bearing names she'd never heard before, though she supposed they must be family, in some distant past before she had been born. Alice loved to stroll through the graveyard, to pick the funereal flowers from old grassy knolls where someone dead most certainly must lie beneath. For her, there was always adventure in a graveyard.

Despite her sister's nasty disposition, it would have been a perfectly cloudy, chilly day in her favorite play place had she not been so hungry, for her sister had refused to have tea before angrily bringing Alice outside. Tea and a sandwich would be nice. Perhaps a nice meat pie, if the cook could be bothered to bake one up. For their cook made the best meat pies in the world and Alice could think of no better meal than a delicious hot meat pie.

As if being ravenous wasn't enough, now her sister was also refusing her the joy of perusing the ancient stones, and had hold of her arm while she read such dull material. Once or twice she had peeped into the book her sister was reading, but it had no pictures or conversations in it, "and what is the use of a book," thought Alice "without pictures or conversation?"

So she was considering in her own mind (as well as she could, for the chill of the bleak day made her feel very sleepy and stupid) whether the plea-sure of making a daisy chain would be worth the trouble of getting up and picking the daisies, when suddenly a sleek Black Rat with shining dark eyes ran straight from a nearby tomb and quite close by her.

There was nothing so *very* remarkable in that; nor did Alice think it so *very* much out of the way to hear the Black Rat say to itself, "Oh dear! Oh dear! I shall be late!" (when she thought it over afterwards, it occurred to her that she ought to have wondered at this, but at the time it all seemed quite natural); but, when the Black Rat actually *took a watch out of its waistcoat-pocket*, and looked at it, and then hurried on, Alice broke from her sister's grip and started to her feet, for it flashed across her mind that she had never before seen a rat with either a waistcoat-pocket, or a watch to take out of it, and, burning with curiosity, she ran across the graveyard after it, despite her sister's angry yells for her to come straight back to her this instant, and fortunately was just in time to see it pop down into a gaping open grave. Clods of gray dirt sat all around its edge and a displeasing smell seemed to waft up from it.

For a moment, Alice stood beside the grave, her sister's voice far away and still frightening for all the distance, deciding whether she'd dare jump in after the strange Black Rat. In another moment, down went Alice after it, hardly considering how in the world she was to get out again.

Then she was tumbling forward into the stinking, black grave which went straight on like a tunnel for some way, and then dipped suddenly down, so suddenly that Alice had not a moment to think about stopping herself before she found herself falling down and down. On the way down, she hit her head upon the leaning tombstone, and tears filled her eyes for a moment as she tumbled forward.

Either the grave was very deep, or she fell very slowly, for she had plenty of time as she went down to look about her and to wonder what was going to happen next. First, she checked the smarting place on her head and pulled back a small hand coated with bright red blood. Her head hurt quite a bit, but as there was nothing to do but cry or get along with her adventure, she chose to stifle her tears and smile through the pain bravely. Then she tried to look down and make out what she was coming to, but it was too dark to see anything; then she looked at the sides of the deep, deep grave, and noticed that they were filled with strange and frightening things. In some places, she could see rotting bones poking from the dark soil; in others skulls leered at her as she fell by them, missing teeth giving silent voice perhaps to warn her back from what lie at the bottom of the grave. It made her feel quite out of sorts to see such emblems of death sitting so close next to her.

"Well!" thought Alice to herself, "after such a fall as this, I shall think nothing of tumbling down stairs! How brave they'll all think me at home! Why, I wouldn't say anything about it, even if I fell off the top of the house!" (Which was very likely true.)

Down, down, down. Would the fall *never* come to an end! "I wonder how many miles I've fallen by this time?" she said aloud. "I must be getting somewhere near the center of the earth. Let me see: that would be four thousand miles down, I think—" (for, you see, Alice had learnt several things of this sort in her lessons in the schoolroom, and though this was not a *very* good opportunity for showing off her knowledge, as there was no one to listen to her, still it was good practice to say it over) "—yes, that's about the right distance— but then I wonder what Latitude or Longitude I've got to?" (Alice had no idea what Latitude was, or Longitude either, but thought they were nice grand words to say.)

Presently she began again. "I wonder if I shall fall right *through* the earth! How funny it'll seem to come out among the people that walk with their heads downward! The Antipathies, I think—" (she was rather glad there WAS no one listening, this time, as it didn't sound at all the right word) "—but I shall have to ask them what the name of the country is, you know. Please, Ma'am, is this

New Zealand or Australia?" (And she tried to curt-sey as she spoke—fancy *curtseying* as you're falling through the air! Do you think you could manage it?) "And what an ignorant little girl she'll think me for asking! No, it'll never do to ask: perhaps I shall see it written up somewhere."

Down, down, down. The pain in her head had turned into a deep throb, but she continued to ignore it and held in her tears some more. There was nothing else to do, so Alice soon began talk-ing again. "Dinah'll miss me very much tonight, I should think!" (Dinah was the cat.) "I hope they'll remember her saucer of milk at tea-time. Dinah my dear! I wish you were down here with me! There are no mice in the air, I'm afraid, but you might catch a bat, and that's very like a mouse, you know. But do cats eat bats, I wonder?" And here Alice began to get rather sleepy, and went on saying to herself, in a dreamy sort of way, "Do cats eat bats? Do cats eat bats?" and sometimes, "Do bats eat cats?" for, you see, as she couldn't answer either question, it didn't much matter which way she put it. She felt that she was dozing off, and had just begun to dream that she was walking hand in hand with Dinah, and saying to her very earnestly, "Now, Dinah, tell me the truth: did you ever eat a bat?" when suddenly, thump! thump! down she came upon a heap of cold sodden earth that smelled of dead things. Nasty, pale worms writhed throughout the small hill and she hastily threw herself from the dirt, wincing in disgust. Worms and beetles crawled through the sodden earth, clicking and grubbing along at her feet. Was this what a grave was like inside? she wondered. She'd often wondered how the darkness got along without the light of the sun, how things lived; now she had a better idea how the things that lived without light got along.

Alice's head still ached but she decided to ignore it and she looked up, but it was all dark overhead; before her was another long passage, and the Black Rat was still in sight, hurrying down it.

There was not a moment to be lost: away went Alice like the wind, and was just in time to hear it say, as it turned a corner, "Oh my ears and whiskers, how late it's getting!" She was close behind it when she turned the corner, but the Rat was no longer to be seen: she found herself in a long, low hall, which was lit up by a row of dim, flickering lamps that seemed to cast off a cold light hanging from the roof.

There were doors all round the hall, but they were all locked; and when Alice had been all the way down one side and up the other, trying every door, she walked sadly down the middle, wondering how she was ever to get out again.

Suddenly she came upon a little three-legged table, all made of solid glass; there was nothing on it except a tiny golden key, and Alice's first thought was that it might belong to one of the doors of the hall; but, alas! either the locks were too large, or the key was too small, but at any rate it would not open any of them. However, on the second time round, she came upon a low black curtain she had not noticed before, and behind it was a little door about fifteen inches high: she tried the little golden key in the lock, and to her great delight it fitted!

Alice opened the door and found that it led into a small passage, not much larger than a rat-hole: she knelt down and looked along the passage into the grandest graveyard you ever saw. How she longed to get out of that dark hall, and wander about among the tall upright headstones and weathered and ancient tombs, to lay amongst the weedy distance and the wood beyond. She was sure adventure could be had in a wood so dark and foreboding, but she could not even get her bloody, throbbing head though the doorway; "and even if my head would go through," thought poor Alice, "it would be of very little use without my shoulders. Oh, how I wish I could shut up like a telescope! I think I could, if I only knew how to begin." For, you see, so many out-of-the-way things had happened lately, that Alice had begun to think that very few things indeed were really impossible.

There seemed to be no use in waiting by the little door, so she went back to the table, half hoping she might find another key on it, or at any rate a book of rules for shutting people up like telescopes: this time she found a little bottle on it, ("which certainly was not here before," said Alice,) and round the neck of the bottle was a paper label, with the words "*Drink me*" beautifully printed on it in large letters.

It was all very well to say "Drink me," but the wise little Alice was not going to do *that* in a hurry. "No, I'll look first," she said, "and see whether it's marked 'poison' or not"; for she had read several nice little histories about children who had got burnt, and eaten up by wild beasts and other unpleasant things, all because they *would* not remember the simple rules their friends had taught them: such as, that a red-hot poker will burn you if you hold it too long; and that if you cut your finger *very* deeply with a knife, it usually bleeds; and she had never forgotten that, if you drink much from a bottle marked "poison," it is almost certain to disagree with you, sooner or later.

However, this bottle was *not* marked "poison," so Alice ventured to taste it, and finding it very nice (it had, in fact, a sort of mixed flavor of cherry-tart, custard, pineapple, roast turkey, toffee, and hot buttered toast), she very soon finished it off. "What a curious feeling!" said Alice. "I must be shutting up like a telescope."

And so it was indeed: she was now only ten inches high, and her face brightened up at the thought that she was now the right size for going through the little door into that lovely graveyard. First, however, she waited for a few minutes to see if she was going to shrink any further: she felt a little nervous about this; "for it might end, you know," said Alice to herself, "in my going out altogether, like a candle. I wonder what I should be like then?" And she tried to fancy what the flame of a candle is like after the candle is blown out, for she could not remember ever having seen such a thing.

After a while, finding that nothing more happened, she decided on going into the graveyard at once; but, alas for poor Alice! when she got to the door, she found she had forgotten the little golden key, and when she went back to the table for it, she found she could not possibly reach it: she could see it quite plainly through the glass, and she tried her best to climb up one of the legs of the table, but it was too slippery; and when she had tired herself out with trying, the poor little thing sat down and finally cried. Her head hurt dreadfully and she felt so tired and frustrated.

"Come, there's no use in crying like that!" said Alice to herself, rather sharply; "I advise you to leave off this minute!" She generally gave herself very good advice, (though she very seldom followed it) and sometimes she scolded herself so severely as to bring tears into her eyes; and once she remembered trying to box her own ears for having cheated herself in a game of croquet she was playing against herself, for this curious child was very fond of pretending to be two people. "But it's no use now," thought poor Alice, "to pretend to be two people! Why, there's hardly enough of me left to make *one* respectable person!"

Soon her eye fell on a little glass box that was lying under the table: she opened it, and found in it a very small cake, on which the words "*Eat me*" were beautifully marked in currants. "Well, I'll eat it," said Alice, "and if it makes me grow larger, I can reach the key; and if it makes me grow smaller, I can creep under the door; so either way I'll get into the graveyard and the woods, and I don't care which happens!"

She ate a little bit, and said anxiously to herself, "Which way? Which way?" holding her hand on the top of her seeping head to feel which way it was growing, and she was quite surprised to find that she remained the same size: to be sure, this generally happens when one eats cake, but Alice had got so much into the way of expecting nothing but out-of-the-way things to happen, that it seemed quite dull and stupid for life to go on in the common way.

So she set to work, and very soon finished off the cake.

CHAPTER II

THE POOL OF BLOOD

CURIOUSER and curiouser!" cried Alice (she was so much surprised, that for the moment she quite forgot how to speak good English); "now I'm opening out like the largest telescope that ever was! Good-bye, feet!" (for when she looked down at her feet, they seemed to be almost out of sight, they were getting so far off). "Oh, my poor little feet, I wonder who will put on your shoes and stockings for you now, dears? I'm sure *I* shan't be able! I shall be a great deal too far off to trouble myself about you: you must manage the best way you can—but I must be kind to them," thought Alice, "or perhaps they won't walk the way I want to go! Let me see: I'll give them a new pair of boots every Christmas."

And she went on planning to herself how she would manage it. "They must go by the carrier," she thought; "and how funny it'll seem, sending presents to one's own feet! And how odd the directions will look!

> *Alice's right foot, Esq.*
> *Hearthrug,*
> *Near the fender,*
> (*With Alice's love*).

Oh dear, what nonsense I'm talking!"

Just then her already aching, bleeding head struck against the roof of the hall: in fact she was now more than nine feet high, and she at once took up the little golden key and hurried off to the little door.

Poor Alice! It was as much as she could do, lying down on one side, to look through into the garden with one eye; but to get through was more hopeless than ever: she sat down and began to cry again. "You ought to be ashamed of yourself," said Alice, "a great girl like you," (she might well say this), "to go on crying in this way! Stop this moment, I tell you!" But she went on all the same. But the bump to her head had really started the blood flowing now and soon she was shedding gallons of warm, red blood, until there was a large pool all round her, about four inches deep and reaching half down the hall.

After a time she heard a little pattering of feet in the distance, and she hastily dried her eyes, wiping the blood from her face (strangely enough she no longer felt any pain at all; it was as if that last bump had settled the matter of whether she *must* feel pain), to see what was coming. It was the Black Rat returning, splendidly dressed, with a pair of white kid gloves in one hand and a large fan in the other: he came trotting along in a great hurry, muttering to himself as he came, "Oh! the Duchess, the Duchess! Oh! won't she be savage if I've kept her waiting!" Alice felt so desperate that she was ready to ask help of any one; so, when the Rat came near her, she began, in a low, timid voice, "If you please, sir—" The Rat started violently, dropped the white kid gloves and the fan, and scurried away into the darkness as hard as he could go.

Alice took up the fan and gloves, and, as the hall was very hot, she kept fanning herself all the time she went on talking: "Dear, dear! How queer everything is to-day! And yesterday things went on just as usual. I wonder if I've been changed in the night? Let me think: was I the same when I got up this morning? I almost think I can remember feeling a little different. But if I'm not the same, the next question is, Who in the world am I? Ah, *that's* the great puzzle!" And she began thinking over all the children she knew that were of the same age as herself, to see if she could have been changed for any of them.

"I'm sure I'm not Ada," she said, "for her hair goes in such long ringlets, and mine doesn't go in ringlets at all; and I'm sure I can't be Mabel, for I know all sorts of things, and she, oh! She knows such a very little! Besides, *she's* she, and

I'm I, and—oh dear, how puzzling it all is! I'll try if I know all the things I used to know. Let me see: four times five is twelve, and four times six is thirteen, and four times seven is—oh dear! I shall never get to twenty at that rate! However, the Multiplication Table doesn't signify: let's try Geography. London is the capital of Paris, and Paris is the capital of Rome, and Rome—no, *that's* all wrong, I'm certain! I must have been changed for Mabel! I'll try and say '*How doth the little*—'" and she crossed her hands on her lap as if she were saying lessons, and began to repeat it, but her voice sounded hoarse and strange, and she felt oddly cold and hungry (but hungry for what? she wondered), and the words did not come the same as they used to do:

> "How doth the little crocodile
> Improve his shining tail,
> And pour the waters of the Nile
> On every golden scale!

"How cheerfully he seems to grin,
How neatly spread his claws,
And welcome little fishes in
With gently smiling jaws!"

"I'm sure those are not the right words," said poor Alice. She could hardly think of anything but how she was ravenous for something she could not name. And her eyes filled with tears again as she went on, "I must be Mabel after all, for she eats and eats all the time and hardly has time to play, and I shall have to go and live in that poky little house, and have next to no toys to play with, and oh! ever so many lessons to learn! No, I've made up my mind about it; if I'm Mabel, I'll stay down here! It'll be no use their putting their heads down and saying 'Come up again, dear!' I shall only look up and say 'Who am I then? Tell me that first, and then, if I like being that person, I'll come up: if not, I'll stay down here till I'm somebody else'— but, oh dear!" cried Alice, with a sudden burst of tears, "I do wish they *would* put their heads down! I am so *very* tired of being all alone here!"

As she said this she looked down at her hands, and was surprised to see that she had put on one of the Rat's little white kid gloves while she was talking. "How *can* I have done that?" she thought. "I must be growing small again." She got up and went to the table to measure herself by it, and found that, as nearly as she could guess, she was now about two feet high, and was going on shrinking rapidly: she soon found out that the cause of this was the fan she was holding, and she dropped it hastily, just in time to avoid shrinking away altogether.

"That *was* a narrow escape!" said Alice, a good deal frightened at the sudden change, but very glad to find herself still in existence; "and now for the graveyard!" and she ran with all speed back to the little door: but, alas! the little door was shut again, and the little golden key was lying on the glass table as before, "and things are worse than ever," thought the poor child, "for I never was so small as this before, never! And I declare it's too bad, that it is! But at least my head no longer pains me. If only I could figure out what I'm so hungry for, though."

As she said these words her foot slipped, and in another moment, splash! she was up to her chin in salty, warm blood. Her first idea was that she had somehow fallen into the sea, "and in that case I can go back by railway," she said to herself. (Alice had been to the seaside once in her life, and had come to the general conclusion, that wherever you go to on the English coast you find a number of bathing machines in the sea, some children digging in the sand with wooden spades, then a row of lodging houses, and behind them a railway station.) However, she soon made out that she was in the pool of blood which she had bled when she was nine feet high.

"I wish I hadn't bled so much!" said Alice, as she swam about, trying to find her way out. "I shall be punished for it now, I suppose, by being drowned in my own blood! That *will* be a queer thing, to be sure! However, everything is queer to-day."

Just then she heard something splashing about in the blood pool a little way off, and she swam nearer to make out what it was: at first she thought it must be a walrus or hippopotamus, but then she remembered how small she was now, and she soon made out that it was only a mouse that had slipped in like herself.

"Would it be of any use, now," thought Alice, "to speak to this mouse? Everything is so out-of-the-way down here, that I should think very likely it can talk: at any rate, there's no harm in trying." So she began: "O Mouse, do you know the way out of this pool? I am very tired of swimming about here, O Mouse!" Alice thought this must be the right way of speaking to a mouse: she had never done such a thing before, but she remembered having seen in her brother's Latin Grammar, "A mouse— of a mouse—to a mouse—a mouse—O mouse!" The Mouse looked at her rather inquisitively, and seemed to her to wink with one of its little eyes, but it said nothing.

"Perhaps it doesn't understand English," thought Alice; "I daresay it's a French mouse, come over with William the Conqueror." (For, with all her knowledge of history, Alice had no very clear notion how long ago anything had happened.) So she began again: "Où est ma chatte?" which was the first sentence in her French lesson-book. The Mouse gave a sudden leap out of the warm blood, and seemed to quiver all over with fright. "Oh, I beg your pardon!" cried Alice hastily, afraid that she had hurt the poor animal's feelings. "I quite forgot you didn't like cats."

"Not like cats!" cried the Mouse, in a shrill, passionate voice. "Would *you* like cats if you were me?"

"Well, perhaps not," said Alice in a soothing tone: "don't be angry about it. And yet I wish I could show you our cat Dinah: I think you'd take a fancy to cats if you could only see her. She is such a dear quiet thing," Alice went on, half to herself, as she swam lazily about in the sticky thick blood, "and she sits purring so nicely by the fire, licking her paws and washing her face—and she is such a nice soft thing to nurse—and she's such a capital one for catching mice—oh, I beg your pardon!" cried Alice again, for this time the Mouse was bristling all over, and she felt certain it must be really offended. "We won't talk about her any more if you'd rather not."

"We indeed!" cried the Mouse, who was trembling down to the end of his tail. "As if I would talk on such a subject! Our family always *hated* cats: nasty, low, vulgar things! Don't let me hear the name again!"

"I won't indeed!" said Alice, in a great hurry to change the subject of conversation. "Are you— are you fond—of—of dogs?" The Mouse did not answer, so Alice went on eagerly: "There is such a nice little dog near our house I should like to show you! A little bright-eyed terrier, you know, with oh, such long curly brown hair! And it'll fetch things when you throw them, and it'll sit up and beg for its dinner, and all sorts of things—I can't remember half of them—and it belongs to a farmer, you know, and he says it's so useful, it's worth a hundred pounds! He says it kills all the rats and—oh dear!" cried Alice in a sorrowful tone, "I'm afraid I've offended it again!" For the Mouse was swimming away from her as hard as it could go, and making quite a commotion in the pool as it went.

But the thought of the frisky dogs snapping little squealing rats in half, gulping down their warm, trembling flesh, got her hungry all over again. She licked her lips and looked after the nice fat little Mouse with new eyes.

So she called softly after it, "Mouse dear! Do come back again, and we won't talk about cats or dogs either, if you don't like them!" When the Mouse heard this, it turned round and swam slowly back to her: its face was quite fat and full looking, Alice thought, and it said in a low trembling voice, "Let us get to the shore, and then I'll tell you my history, and you'll understand why it is I hate cats and dogs."

It was high time to go, for the pool was getting quite crowded with the birds and animals that had fallen into it: there were a Duck and a Dodo, a Lory and an Eaglet, and several other curious creatures. Alice led the way, and the whole party swam to the shore. Along the way, she wondered what each and every one of them might taste like if she were to take a bite—oh, only a little one—at first. Her stomach gave a strange gurgle of agreement.

CHAPTER III

A ZOMBIE-RACE AND A LONG TALE

THEY were indeed a queer-looking party that assembled on the bank—the birds with draggled feathers, the animals with their fur clinging close to them, and all dripping wet, cross, and uncomfortable. All of them were covered in Alice's now cold and congealed blood, which made them even tastier looking to poor hungry Alice.

The first question of course was, how to get dry again: they had a consultation about this, and after a few minutes it seemed quite natural to Alice to find herself talking familiarly with them, as if she had known them all her life. Indeed, she had quite a long argument with the Lory, who at last turned sulky, and would only say, "I am older than you, and must know better"; and this Alice would not allow without knowing how old it was, and, as the Lory positively refused to tell its age, there was no more to be said. Besides, she was afraid to get too close to him to guess his age, for his small little legs were beginning to look quite scrumptious to her. She felt her mouth water at the thought of taking one of his young or old legs—which ever—between her teeth and pulling the warm flesh from it. It was all she could do to move away from him and join the others.

At last the Mouse, who seemed to be a person of authority among them, called out. "Sit down, all of you, and listen to me! *I'll* soon make you dry enough!" They all sat down at once, in a large ring, with the Mouse in the middle. Alice kept her eyes anxiously fixed on it, for she wanted very much to nibble on his tiny tail, to see if it tasted like licorice as she though it might.

"Ahem!" said the Mouse with an important air, "are you all ready? This is the driest thing I know. Silence all round, if you please! 'William the Conqueror, whose cause was favored by the pope, was soon submitted to by the English, who wanted leaders, and had been of late much accustomed to usurpation and conquest. Edwin and Morcar, the earls of Mercia and Northumbria—'"

"Ugh!" said the Lory, with a shiver.

"I beg your pardon!" said the Mouse, frowning, but very politely. "Did you speak?"

"Not I!" said the Lory hastily.

"I thought you did," said the Mouse. "—I proceed. 'Edwin and Morcar, the earls of Mercia and Northumbria, declared for him: and even Stigand, the patriotic archbishop of Canterbury, found it advisable—'"

"Found *what*?" said the Duck.

"Found *it*," the Mouse replied rather crossly: "of course you know what 'it' means."

"I know what 'it' means well enough, when I find a thing," said the Duck: "it's generally a frog or a worm. The question is, what did the archbishop find?"

The Mouse did not notice this question, but hurriedly went on, "'—found it advisable to go with

Edgar Atheling to meet William and offer him the crown. William's conduct at first was moderate. But the insolence of his Normans—' How are you getting on now, my dear?" it continued, turning to Alice as it spoke.

"Hungry—I mean as wet as ever," said Alice in a melancholy tone: "it doesn't seem to dry me at all."

The Dodo looked her over humorlessly, his little eyes staring at her wilting hair and pale skin.

Alice's brow furrowed in aggravation and she was about to say something, but as she opened her mouth to speak, one of her teeth tumbled from her mouth, and she was so disturbed to see it fall to the ground, she kept her mouth close-lipped from that moment on. Her hair was falling out, and now her teeth, too? Alice felt a chill wash over her that could not be blamed solely on being soaking wet.

"In that case," said the Dodo solemnly, rising to its feet, "I move that the meeting adjourn, for the immediate adoption of more energetic remedies—"

"Speak English!" said the Eaglet. "I don't know

the meaning of half those long words, and, what's more, I don't believe you do either!" And the Eaglet bent down its head to hide a smile: some of the other birds tittered audibly.

"What I was going to say," said the Dodo in an offended tone, "was, that the best thing to get us dry would be a Zombie-race."

"What *is* a Zombie-race?" said Alice; not that she wanted much to know, but the Dodo had paused as if it thought that *somebody* ought to speak, and no one else seemed inclined to say anything.

"Why," said the Dodo, "the best way to explain it is to do it." (And, as you might like to try the thing yourself, some winter day, I will tell you how the Dodo managed it.)

First it marked out a race-course, in a sort of circle, ("the exact shape doesn't matter," it said,) and then all the party were placed along the course, here and there. There was no "One, two, three, and away," but they began stumbling around in circles, eyes rolled to the backs of their heads, arms

41

held out, making low moaning sounds. It was not easy to know when the race was over. However, when they had been moaning and staggering around for half an hour or so, and were quite dry again, the Dodo suddenly called out "The race is over!" and they all crowded round it, panting, and asking, "But who has won?"

This question the Dodo could not answer without a great deal of thought, and it sat for a long time with one finger pressed upon its forehead (the position in which you usually see Shakespeare, in the pictures of him), while the rest waited in silence. At last the Dodo said, "*Everybody* has won, and all must have prizes."

"But who is to give the prizes?" quite a chorus of voices asked.

"Why, *she*, of course," said the Dodo, pointing to Alice with one finger; and the whole party at once crowded round her, calling out in a confused way, "Prizes! Prizes!"

Alice had no idea what to do, and in despair she

put her hand in her pocket, and pulled out a box of comfits, (luckily the blood had not got into it), and handed them round as prizes. There was exactly one a-piece all round.

"But she must have a prize herself, you know," said the delicious-looking little Mouse.

"Of course," the tasty Dodo replied very gravely. "What else have you got in your pocket?" he went on, turning to Alice.

"Only a thimble," said Alice sadly, still thinking how much she would like to eat her new friends. She could not decide if she would do so with sauce or not. She wasn't sure it mattered much as she could not think of a polite way to ask them for a taste of their flesh.

"Hand it over here," said the Dodo.

Then they all crowded round her once more, while the Dodo solemnly presented the thimble, saying, "We beg your acceptance of this elegant thimble"; and, when it had finished this short speech, they all cheered.

"If only the Queen herself was here to present it, perhaps it would have more meaning," said the Eaglet.

"More meaning, indeed," humphed the Dodo. "Besides, I feel sure not everyone here would appreciate a visit from the Red Queen." And he looked most sternly at Alice.

Alice thought the whole thing very absurd, but they all looked so grave that she did not dare to laugh; and, as she could not think of anything to say, she simply bowed, and took the thimble, looking as solemn as she could. Perhaps sauce would be best, she thought, licking her lips again.

The next thing was to eat the comfits: this caused some noise and confusion, as the large birds complained that they could not taste theirs, and the small ones choked and had to be patted on the back. Much to Alice's despair, no one died, so that she could ask to have a taste before burial. However, it was over at last, and they sat down again in a ring, and begged the Mouse to tell them something more.

"You promised to tell me your history, you know," said Alice, "and why it is you hate—C and D," she added in a whisper, half afraid that it would be offended again.

"Mine is a long and a sad tale!" said the Mouse, turning to Alice, and sighing.

"It *is* a long tail, certainly," said Alice, looking down with wonder at the Mouse's tail; "but why do you call it sad? I think it looks wonderfully delicious." And she kept on puzzling about it while the Mouse was speaking, so that her idea of the tale was something like this:

> "Fury said to a
>   mouse, That he
>   met in the
>   house,
>   'Let us
>   both go to
>   law: I will
>   prosecute
>   you.—Come,

I'll take no
denial; We
must have a
trial: For
really this
morning I've
nothing
to do.'
Said the
mouse to the
cur, 'such
a trial,
dear Sir,
With
no jury
or judge,
would be
wasting
our
breath.'
'I'll be
judge, I'll
be jury,'
said
cunning
old Fury:
'I'll
try the
whole
cause,
and
condemn
you
to
death.'"

"You are not attending!" said the Mouse to Alice severely. "What are you thinking of?"

"I beg your pardon," said Alice very humbly: "you had got to the fifth bend, I think?"

"I had *not*!" cried the Mouse, sharply and very angrily.

"A knot!" said Alice, always ready to make herself useful, and looking anxiously about her. "Oh, do let me help to undo it!" Perhaps she could nibble a little and he would not notice if only a tiny bit of his tail was missing.

"I shall do nothing of the sort," said the Mouse, getting up and walking away. "You insult me by talking such nonsense!"

"I didn't mean it!" pleaded poor Alice, trying to hide the ravenous hunger in her starving eyes. "But you're so easily offended, you know!"

The Mouse only growled in reply.

"Please come back and finish your story!" Alice called after it; and the others all joined in chorus, "Yes, please do!" but the Mouse only shook its head impatiently, and walked a little quicker.

"What a pity it wouldn't stay!" sighed the Lory, as soon as it was quite out of sight; and an old Crab took the opportunity of saying to her daughter "Ah, my dear! Let this be a lesson to you never to lose *your* temper!" "Hold your tongue, Ma!" said the young Crab, a little snappishly. "You're enough to try the patience of an oyster!"

"I wish I had our Dinah here, I know I do!" said Alice aloud, addressing nobody in particular. "She'd soon fetch the delicious little Mouse back! Or if not, I'm sure Dinah would allow me a little nibble of her dainty paw to ease my hunger."

"And who is Dinah, if I might venture to ask the question?" said the Lory.

Alice replied eagerly, for she was always ready to talk about her pet: "Dinah's our cat. And she's such a capital one for catching mice you can't think! And oh, I wish you could see her after the birds! Why, she'll eat a little bird as soon as look at it!" Alice felt her tummy rumble at the thought of a nice plump bird—preferably uncooked and still alive.

This speech caused a remarkable sensation among the party. Some of the birds hurried off at once: one old Magpie began wrapping itself up very carefully, remarking, "I really must be getting home; the night-air doesn't suit my throat!" and a Canary called out in a trembling voice to its children, "Come away, my dears! It's high time you were all in bed!" On various pretexts they all moved off, and Alice was soon left alone.

"I wish I hadn't mentioned Dinah!" she said to herself in a melancholy tone. "Nobody seems to like her, down here, and I'm sure she's the best cat in the world! Oh, my dear Dinah! I wonder if I shall ever see you any more!" And here poor Alice began to cry again, for she felt very lonely and low-spirited, and her hunger was just becoming too much to bear, she was sure. In a little while, however, she again heard a little pattering of footsteps in the distance, and she looked up eagerly, half hoping that the tasty tiny Mouse had changed his mind, and was coming back to let her chew a bit of his tail.

CHAPTER IV

THE BLACK RAT SENDS IN THE UNDEAD

It was the Black Rat, trotting slowly back again, and looking anxiously about as it went, as if it had lost something; and she heard it muttering to itself, "The Duchess! The Duchess! Oh my dear paws! Oh my fur and whiskers! She'll get me executed, as sure as ferrets are ferrets! Where *can* I have dropped them, I wonder?" Alice guessed in a moment that it was looking for the fan and the pair of white kid gloves, and she very good-naturedly began hunting about for them, but they were nowhere to be seen— everything seemed to have changed since her swim in the blood pool, and the great hall, with the glass table and the little door, had vanished completely.

Very soon the Rat noticed Alice, as she went hunting about, and called out to her in an angry tone, "Why, Mary Ann, what *are* you doing out here? Run home this moment, and fetch me a pair of gloves and a fan! Quick, now!" And Alice was so much frightened that she ran off at once in the direction it pointed to, without trying to explain the mistake it had made.

"He took me for his housemaid," she said to herself as she ran. "How surprised he'll be when he finds out who I am! But I'd better take him his fan and gloves—that is, if I can find them."

As she said this, she came upon a neat little house, on the door of which was a tarnished and barely readable brass plate with the name "B. RAT" engraved upon it. She went in without knocking, and hurried upstairs, in great fear lest she should meet the real Mary Ann, and be turned out of the house before she had found the fan and gloves.

"How queer it seems," Alice said to herself, "to be going messages for a Rat! I suppose Dinah'll be sending me on messages next!" And she began fancying the sort of thing that would happen: 'Miss Alice! Come here directly, and get ready for your walk!'

'Coming in a minute, nurse! But I've got to see that the mouse doesn't get out.' Only I don't think," Alice went on, "that they'd let Dinah stop in the house if it began ordering people about like that!"

By this time she had found her way into a messy little room, filled with odds and bits of gnawed bone and strings of grave hair, rotting flowers, and such, with a table in the window, and on it (as she had hoped) a fan and two or three pairs of tiny white kid gloves: she took up the fan and a pair of the gloves, and was just going to leave the room, when her eye fell upon a little dark bottle that stood near the looking-glass. There was no label this time with the words "*Drink me*," but nevertheless she uncorked it and put it to her lips. It smelled of roasting meat and cold gravy. "I know *something* interesting is sure to happen," she said to herself, "whenever I eat or drink anything; so I'll just see what this bottle does. I do hope it'll make me grow large again, for really I'm quite tired of being such a tiny little thing!"

It did so indeed, and much sooner than she had expected: before she had drunk half the bottle, she found her head pressing against the ceiling, and had to stoop to save her neck from being broken. She hastily put down the bottle, saying to herself "That's quite enough—I hope I shan't grow any more—As it is, I can't get out at the door—I do wish I hadn't drunk quite so much!"

Alas! it was too late to wish that! She went on growing, and growing, and very soon had to kneel down on the floor: in another minute there was not even room for this, and she tried the effect of lying down with one elbow against the door, and the other arm curled round her head. Her head was smashed into the rotting, gnawed upon bones; wet smelly grave hair tangled up in her fingers and tickled her nose. Still she went on growing, and, as a last resource, she put one arm out of the window, and one foot up the chimney, and said to herself, "Now I can do no more, whatever happens. What *will* become of me?"

Luckily for Alice, the little magic bottle had now had its full effect, and she grew no larger: still it was very uncomfortable, and, as there seemed to be no sort of chance of her ever getting out of the room again, no wonder she felt unhappy.

"It was much pleasanter at home," thought poor Alice, "when one wasn't always growing larger and smaller, and being ordered about by mice and rats. I almost wish I hadn't gone down into that grave looking for adventure—and yet—and yet—it's rather curious, you know, this sort of life! I do wonder what *can* have happened to me! When I used to read fairy-tales, I fancied that kind of thing never happened, and now here I am in the middle of one! There ought to be a book written about me, that there ought! And when I grow up, I'll write one—but I'm grown up now," she added in a sorrowful tone; "at least there's no room to grow up any more *here*."

"But then," thought Alice, "shall I *never* get any older than I am now? That'll be a comfort, one way—never to be an old woman—never to have to watch my hands shrivel up like grandmammy's and my long hair going dry and gray with age— but then—always to have lessons to learn! Oh, I shouldn't like *that*!"

"Oh, you foolish Alice!" she answered herself. "How can you learn lessons in here? Why, there's hardly room for *you*, and no room at all for any lesson-books!"

And so she went on, taking first one side and then the other, and making quite a conversation of it altogether; but after a few minutes she heard a voice outside, and stopped to listen.

"Mary Ann! Mary Ann!" said the voice. "Fetch me my gloves this moment!" Then came a little pattering of feet on the stairs. Alice knew it was the Rat coming to look for her, and she trembled till she shook the house, quite forgetting that she was now about a thousand times as large as the Rat, and had no reason to be afraid of it.

Presently the Black Rat came up to the door, and

tried to open it; but, as the door opened inwards, and Alice's elbow was pressed hard against it, that attempt proved a failure. Alice heard it say to itself "Then I'll go round and get in at the window."

"*That* you won't" thought Alice, and, after waiting till she fancied she heard the Rat just under the window, she suddenly spread out her hand, and made a snatch in the air. She did not get hold of anything, but she heard a little shriek and a fall, and a crash of broken glass, from which she concluded that it was just possible it had fallen into a cucumber-frame, or something of the sort.

Next came an angry voice—the Rat's—"Pat! Pat! Where are you?" And then a voice she had never heard before. "Sure then I'm here! Digging for fresh bodies, yer honor! Must have something to eat, don't we, now?"

"Digging for fresh bodies, indeed!" said the Rat angrily. "And what would the Queen say to that, do you think? You know the rules! Here! Come and help me out of *this*!" (Sounds of more broken glass.)

"Now tell me, Pat, what's that in the window?"

"Sure, it's an arm, yer honor!" (He pronounced it "arrum.") A right tasty looking one, too. Not too dead yet. Should make fur a mighty fin' meal, yer honor."

"An arm, you goose! Who ever saw one that size? Good for gnawing or not, it fills the whole window!"

"Sure, it does, yer honor: but it's an arm for all that."

"Well, it's got no business there, at any rate: go and take it away!"

There was a long silence after this, and Alice could only hear whispers now and then; such as, "Sure, I don't like it, yer honor, at all, at all!" "Do as I tell you, you coward!" and at last she spread out her hand again, and made another snatch in the air. Eat my arm, indeed, she thought testily. This time there were *two* little shrieks, and more sounds of broken glass. "What a number of cucumber-frames there must be!" thought Alice. "I wonder what they'll do next! As for pulling me out of the window, I only wish they *could*! I'm sure I don't want to stay in here any longer!"

She waited for some time without hearing anything more: at last came a rumbling of little cartwheels, and the sound of a good many voices all talking together: she made out the words: "Where's the other ladder?—Why, I hadn't to bring but one; Bill's got the other—Bill! fetch it here, lad!—Here, put 'em up at this corner—No, tie 'em together first—they don't reach half high enough yet—Oh! they'll do well enough; don't be particular—Here, Bill! catch hold of this rope— Will the roof bear?—Mind that loose slate—Oh, it's coming down! Heads below!" (a loud crash)— "Now, who did that?—It was Bill, I fancy—He don't look too good, yer honor—Who's to go down the chimney?—Nay, *I* shan't! *You* do it!— *That* I won't, then!—Bill, dead or not, is to go down—Here, Bill! the master says you're to go down the chimney!"

There came a low, terrified moan from what she

thought must be Bill, whoever he was. Something was sent clumsily up the ladder.

"Oh! So Bill's got to come down the chimney, has he?" said Alice to herself. "Why, they seem to put everything upon Bill! I wouldn't be in Bill's place for a good deal: this fireplace is narrow, to be sure; but I *think* I can kick a little!"

She drew her foot as far down the chimney as she could, and waited till she heard a little animal (she couldn't guess of what sort it was) scratching and scrambling about in the chimney close above her. There came an altogether close smell of something that had been left in the sun too long, something overly ripe, fleshy, and dead: then, saying to herself "This is Bill," she gave one sharp kick, and waited to see what would happen next.

The first thing she heard was a general chorus of "There goes Bill!" then the Rat's voice along— "Catch him, you by the hedge!" then silence, and then another confusion of voices—"Hold up his head—How was it, old fellow? What happened to you? Tell us all about it!"

Last came a little moaning voice and some very unpleasant curses from the others. "Hold off, hold off! Don't let him bite you!" ("That's Bill," thought Alice.)

The body digger replied for the dead Bill. "All I know is something sprung him like a Jack-in-the-box, and up he goes like a sky-rocket!"

"So he did, old fellow!" said the others.

"We must burn the house down!" said the Rat's voice; and Alice called out as loud as she could, "If you do, I'll eat you!"

There was a dead silence instantly, and Alice thought to herself, "I wonder what they *will* do next! If they had any sense, they'd take the roof off." After a minute or two, they began moving about again, and Alice heard the Rat say, "A barrowful will do, to begin with."

"A barrowful of *what*?" thought Alice; but she had not long to doubt, for the next moment a shower of little pebbles came rattling in at the window, and some of them hit her in the face. "I'll put a stop to this," she said to herself, and shouted out, "You'd better not do that again!" which produced another dead silence.

Alice noticed with some surprise that the pebbles were all turning into little cakes as they lay on the floor, and a bright idea came into her head. "If I eat one of these cakes," she thought, "it's sure to make *some* change in my size; and as it can't possibly make me larger, it must make me smaller, I suppose."

And although what she really wanted was a nice tasty hunk of red meat, she swallowed one of the cakes, and was delighted to find that she began shrinking directly. As soon as she was small enough to get through the door, she ran out of the house, and found quite a crowd of little animals and birds waiting outside. The poor little dead Lizard, Bill, was in the middle, being held down by two guinea-pigs, who were trying to avoid his snapping teeth.

"We *must* get a collar for poor dead Bill," said the Black Rat.

"Oh, not the collar, yer honor," said one of the guinea pigs in a woeful tone. "Surely we can hide 'im out like. No need to report it to the Queen."

The Black Rat waved a distracted hand at his servant. "You know the rules as well as I do. All dead must be reported to the Red Queen and *must* be collared. If you want to risk your own head, that's fine by me, my good man. But as this happened in my house, we will follow the letter of the law. I happen to like my whiskers sitting above my neck, you know."

And with that he turned away to find Alice was watching them.

They all made a rush at Alice the moment she appeared; but she ran off as hard as she could, and soon found herself safe in a thick wood. She wondered if this was the same wood she had seen from the little door before. It certainly looked dark and foreboding enough. No birds gathered in its branches, and she could only see small red eyes peeking from the thick underbrush within. But she had wanted adventure; and surely the wood had to be better than rats and other animals that wanted to eat her arm.

"The first thing I've got to do," said Alice to herself, as she wandered about in the deep dark wood, hearing only her own footsteps crunching in the dead leaves scattered across the shadowy forest floor, "is to grow to my right size again; and the second thing is to find my way into that lovely graveyard. I think that will be the best plan."

It sounded an excellent plan, no doubt, and very neatly and simply arranged; the only difficulty was, that she had not the smallest idea how to set about it; and while she was peering about anxiously among the trees, a little sharp bark just over her head made her look up in a great hurry.

An enormous dog, its head like a sharply-angled rock, two flint coals for eyes staring eagerly at her, was stretching out one massive, taloned paw, trying to get at her. "Oh my!" said Alice, in a terrified tone, and she tried to shoo it away; but she was terribly frightened all the time at the thought that it might be hungry, in which case it would be very likely to eat her up in spite of all her hopeful shooing.

Hardly knowing what she did, she picked up a little bit of rotting bone under a huge dark tree root, and held it out to the savage dog; whereupon it jumped into the air off all its feet at once, with a yelp of hunger, and rushed at the bone, worrying the bits of decaying flesh upon it; then Alice dodged behind the great tree trunk, to keep herself from being run over; and the moment she appeared on the other side, the growling animal made another rush at her, and tumbled head over heels in its hurry to get hold of her; then Alice, thinking it was very like having a game of play with a cart-horse, and expecting every moment to be trampled under its feet, ran round the twisted tree again; then the monstrous dog began a series of short charges at her, running a very little way forwards each time and a long way back, and barking hoarsely all the while, till at last it sat down a good way off and began to chew upon the rotting bone in earnest, its great eyes half shut.

This seemed to Alice a good opportunity for making her escape; so she set off at once, and ran till she was quite tired and out of breath, and till the animal's gnawing sounded quite faint in the distance.

"That was close!" said Alice, as she leant against a thin sapling that felt dry and cancerous to her touch. A fairy circle of stinking toadstools, all pale and striped with red and brown, were spread round the trees near her, some quite large, in fact, big enough for her to sleep beneath if she ever wanted to sleep in such a musty and frightening place. "I might have liked to take a bite of him, instead, if I'd only been the right size to do it! Oh dear! I'd nearly forgotten that I've got to grow up again! Let me see—how *is* it to be managed? I suppose I ought to eat or drink something or other; but the great question is, what?"

The great question certainly was, what? Alice looked all round her at the tall foreboding trees, all dark and shadowed within their vast skeletal branches but she did not see anything that looked like the right thing to eat or drink under the circumstances. There was a large mushroom growing near her, about the same height as herself; and when she had looked under it, and on both sides of it, and behind it, it occurred to her that she might as well look and see what was on the top of it.

She stretched herself up on tiptoe, and peeped over the edge of the pale, smelly mushroom, and her eyes immediately met those of a large black wurm, that was sitting on the top with its arms folded, quietly supping on a freshly dismembered human ear which it had stolen from the nearby graveyard, and taking not the smallest notice of her or of anything else.

CHAPTER V

ADVICE FROM THE CONQUEROR WURM

THE Wurm and Alice looked at each other for some time in silence. The Conqueror Wurm's body was long and segmented, and the color of wet ash, and smelled somewhat like a dead mouse that Dinah had once brought home to lie at her feet last year. The mouse, all rotting flesh and patchy gray fur, had been dead for quite some time. The Wurm smelled as if it had as well. Or perhaps, Alice thought, it's what it chooses to eat that makes it smell so badly.

At last the Wurm took the half-chewed human ear out of its mouth, and addressed her in a languid, sleepy voice. "Who are *you*?" said the Wurm.

This was not an encouraging opening for a conversation. Alice replied, rather shyly, "I—I hardly know, sir, just at present—at least I know who I *was* when I got up this morning, but I think I must have been changed several times since then."

"What do you mean by that?" said the Wurm sternly. "Explain yourself!"

"I can't explain *myself*, I'm afraid, sir," said Alice, "because I'm not myself, you see."

"I don't see," said the Wurm.

"I feel strangely cold all the time and I'm so dreadfully hungry for the bits and pieces of other living things. I'm afraid I can't put it more clearly," Alice replied very politely, "for I can't understand it myself to begin with; and being so many different sizes in a day is very confusing."

"It isn't," said the Wurm, "hard to explain in the least. Quite natural here, young lady."

"Well, perhaps you haven't found it so yet," said Alice; "but when you have to turn into a chrysalis—you will some day, you know—and then after that into a butterfly, I should think you'll feel it a little queer, won't you?"

"Not a bit," said the Wurm, writhing its long gray body into a loop so to better face Alice.

"Well, perhaps your feelings may be different," said Alice; "all I know is, I feel very queer indeed. Not myself."

"You!" said the Conqueror Wurm contemptuously. "Who are *you*?"

Which brought them back again to the beginning of the conversation. Alice felt a little irritated at the Wurm's making such *very* short remarks, and she drew herself up and said, very gravely, "I think, you ought to tell me who *you* are, first."

"Why?" said the Wurm.

Here was another puzzling question; and as Alice could not think of any good reason, and as the ugly Wurm seemed to be in a *very* unpleasant state of mind, she turned away.

"Come back!" the Wurm called after her, bits of half chewed ear flesh dangling from its small mouth. "I've something important to say!"

This sounded promising, certainly: Alice turned and came back again.

"Keep your temper," said the Wurm.

"Is that all?" said Alice, swallowing down her anger as well as she could.

"No," said the Wurm.

Alice thought she might as well wait, as she had nothing else to do, and perhaps after all it might tell her something worth hearing. For some minutes it munched away on its grotesque dead meal without speaking, but at last it unfolded its arms, took the rotting ear out of its mouth again, and said, "So you think you're changed, do you?"

"I'm afraid I am, sir," said Alice; "I can't remember things as I used—and I don't keep the same size for ten minutes together! And I'm so cold! And starving for warm flesh! I have changed! I know it!" And it was true. Looking at her hands and arms now, she saw they both had a slight blue tinge to them. And her long beautiful hair, which so many people made comments upon, was beginning to come out in stringy handfuls. She would hate to see her reflection now. There was no telling what terrible apparition would look back at her.

"Can't remember *what* things?" said the Wurm.

"Well, I've tried to say '*How doth the little busy bee*,' but it all came different!" Alice replied in a very melancholy voice.

"Repeat, '*You are old, Father William*,'" said the Wurm.

Alice folded her hands, and began:

> "'You are old, Father William,' the young man said,
> 'And your hair has become very white;
> And yet you incessantly stand on your head—
> Do you think, at your age, it is right?'
>
> 'In my youth,' Father William replied to his son,
> 'I feared it might injure the brain;

But, now that I'm perfectly sure I
have none,
Why, I do it again and again.'

'You are old,' said the youth, 'as I men-
tioned before,
And have grown most uncommonly fat;
Yet you turned a back-somersault in at
the door—
Pray, what is the reason of that?'

'In my youth,' said the sage, as he shook
his grey locks,
'I kept all my limbs very supple
By the use of this ointment—one shilling
the box—
Allow me to sell you a couple?'

'You are old,' said the youth, 'and your
jaws are too weak
For anything tougher than suet;

Yet you finished the goose, with the bones
and the beak—
Pray how did you manage to do it?'

'In my youth,' said his father, 'I took to
the law,
And argued each case with my wife;
And the muscular strength, which it gave
to my jaw,
Has lasted the rest of my life.'

'You are old,' said the youth, 'one would
hardly suppose
That your eye was as steady as ever;
Yet you balanced an eel on the end of
your nose—
What made you so awfully clever?'

'I have answered three questions, and that
is enough,'
Said his father; 'don't give yourself airs!

Do you think I can listen all day to
such stuff?
Be off, or I'll kick you down stairs!'"

"That is not said right," said the Wurm.

"Not *quite* right, I'm afraid," said Alice, timidly. "Some of the words have got altered."

"It is wrong from beginning to end," said the Wurm decidedly, and there was silence for some minutes.

The Wurm was the first to speak, as it had almost finished its gory meal of graveyard ear. "What size do you want to be?" it asked.

"Oh, I'm not particular as to size," Alice hastily replied; "only one doesn't like changing so often, you know."

"I *don't* know," said the Wurm.

Alice said nothing: she had never been so much contradicted in her life before, and she felt that she was losing her temper.

"Are you content now?" said the Wurm. It

began to clean its mandibles by rubbing them against its legs and then to its bulbous and shiny gray stomach.

"Well, I should like to be a *little* larger, sir, if you wouldn't mind," said Alice: "three inches is such a wretched height to be."

"It is a very good height indeed!" said the Wurm angrily, rearing itself upright as it spoke (it was exactly three inches high). Its many legs waved in silent fury as it stared down on her with its dead eyes.

For a moment she feared it meant to consume her next, and she backed away in fright. "But I'm not used to it!" pleaded poor Alice in a piteous tone. And she thought to herself, "I wish the creatures wouldn't be so easily offended!"

"You'll get used to it in time," said the Wurm; and it continued to clean its mandibles. "Have you met the Red Queen yet?"

"No, but I've heard such dreadful things about her that I'm sure I'd rather not meet her," said

Alice, crossing her arms across her chest to show she meant business.

The Wurm squirmed a little closer and looked down at her, still working diligently at cleaning its gory mandibles. "You certainly don't want her to see you in that state."

"What state?" asked Alice.

"The state which you are in," it replied.

"I rather thought I was in a land, not a state," she said, quite pleased with her quick and logical wit.

"She's sure to show you, young lady," said the Wurm, not at all impressed with her play on words.

This time Alice waited patiently until it chose to speak again. In a minute or two the Wurm stopped cleaning itself and yawned once or twice, and shook itself. Then it got down off the mushroom, and crawled away in the dead leaves and broken, rotting twigs, merely remarking as it went, "One side will make you grow taller, and the other side will make you grow shorter."

"One side of *what*? The other side of *what*?" thought Alice to herself.

"Of the mushroom," said the Wurm, just as if she had asked it aloud; and in another moment its squirming gray body was out of sight.

Alice remained looking thoughtfully at the mushroom for a minute, trying to make out which were the two sides of it; and as it was perfectly round, she found this a very difficult question. However, at last she stretched her arms round it as far as they would go, and broke off a bit of the edge with each hand.

"And now which is which?" she said to herself, and nibbled a little of the right-hand bit to try the effect: the next moment she felt a violent blow underneath her chin: it had struck her foot!

She was a good deal frightened by this very sudden change, but she felt that there was no time to be lost, as she was shrinking rapidly; so she set to work at once to eat some of the other bit. Her chin was pressed so closely against her foot, that there was hardly room to open her mouth; but she did it at last, and managed to swallow a morsel of the left-hand bit.

"Come, my head's free at last!" said Alice in a tone of delight, which changed into alarm in another moment, when she found that her shoulders were nowhere to be found: all she could see, when she looked down, was an immense length of pale blue neck, which seemed to rise like a stalk out of a tangle of spiny sharp dead branches and autumnal orange and brown leaves that lay far below her.

"What *can* all that brown and orange stuff be?" said Alice. "And where *have* my shoulders got to? And oh, my poor hands, how is it I can't see you?" She was moving them about as she spoke, but no result seemed to follow, except a little shaking among the distant dead leaves.

As there seemed to be no chance of getting her hands up to her head, she tried to get her head down to them, and was delighted to find that her neck would bend about easily in any direction, like a serpent. She had just succeeded in curving it down into a graceful zigzag, and was going to dive in among the dying branches, when a sharp hiss made her draw back in a hurry: a large black raven had flown into her face, and was beating her violently with its long black wings.

"Serpent!" screamed the Raven.

"I'm *not* a serpent!" said Alice indignantly. "Let me alone!"

"Serpent, I say again!" cawed the Raven, but in a more subdued tone, and added with a kind of sob, "I've tried every way, and nothing seems to suit them!"

"I haven't the least idea what you're talking about," said Alice.

"I've tried the roots of trees, and I've tried banks, and I've tried hedges, and I've tried the gravestones and the tombs, too!" the Raven went on, without attending to her; "but those serpents! There's no pleasing them!"

Alice was more and more puzzled, but she thought there was no use in saying anything more till the Raven had finished.

"As if it wasn't trouble enough feeding off the corpses of the dead," said the Raven, flapping its shiny black wings; "but I must be on the look-out for serpents night and day! Why, I haven't had a wink of sleep these three weeks!"

"I'm very sorry you've been annoyed," said Alice, who was beginning to see its meaning. But now as she got closer to the fat bird, she began to think of her hunger again, and her eyes lit up with a most dastardly eagerness. The Raven saw it and backed away on the branch upon which it was sitting. Alice smiled thinly, trying to pretend that she had not been just now thinking what the Raven might taste like if she grabbed it and plucked off its wings.

"And just as I'd taken the highest tree in the wood," continued the Raven, raising its voice to a shriek, "and just as I was thinking I should be free of them at last, they must needs come wriggling down from the sky! Ugh, Serpent!"

"But I'm *not* a serpent, I tell you!" said Alice. "I'm a—I'm a—"

"Well! *What* are you?" said the Raven, beating those delicious looking wings once more in her face. "I can see you're trying to invent something!"

"I—I'm a little girl," said Alice, rather doubtfully, as she remembered the number of changes she had gone through that day.

"A likely story indeed!" said the Raven in a tone of the deepest contempt. "I've seen a good many little girls in my time, both alive and dead, young lady, but never *one* with such a neck as that! No, no! You're a serpent; and there's no use denying it. I suppose you'll be telling me next that you never tasted an egg!"

"I *have* tasted eggs, certainly," said Alice, who was a very truthful child; "but little girls eat eggs quite as much as serpents do, you know." And maybe even nice fat ravens, she thought while licking her dry cold lips.

"I don't believe it," said the Raven; "but if they do, why then they're a kind of serpent, that's all I can say. Oh, why can't the Red Queen take better care of your kind? Why must I be frightened even this far above the ground?"

This was such a new idea to Alice, that she was quite silent for a minute or two, which gave the Raven the opportunity of adding, "You're looking for eggs, I know *that* well enough; and what does it matter to me whether you're a little girl or a serpent?"

"It matters a good deal to *me*," said Alice hastily; "but I'm not looking for eggs, as it happens; and if I was, I shouldn't want *yours*: I don't like them raw."

"Well, be off, then!" said the Raven in a sulky tone, as it settled down again into its nest, and watching her with its beady mistrustful black eyes. Alice crouched down among the trees as well as she could, for her neck kept getting entangled among the skeleton branches, and every now and then she had to stop and untwist it. After a while she remembered that she still held the pieces of mushroom in her hands, and she set to work very carefully, nibbling first at one and then at the other, and growing sometimes taller and sometimes shorter, until she had succeeded in bringing herself down to her usual height.

It was so long since she had been anything near the right size, that it felt quite strange at first; but she got used to it in a few minutes, and began talking to herself, as usual. "Come, there's half my plan done now! How puzzling all these changes are! I'm never sure what I'm going to be, from one minute to another! Now if only I could find some creature willing to give me a bit of itself to eat, I would be just right! However, I've got back to my right size: the next thing is, to get into that beautiful graveyard—how *is* that to be done, I wonder?" As she said this, she came suddenly upon an open place, with a little house in it about four feet high.

"Whoever lives there," thought Alice, "it'll

never do to come upon them *this* size: why, I should frighten them out of their wits!" So she began nibbling at the right-hand bit again, and did not venture to go near the house till she had brought herself down to nine inches high.

CHAPTER VI

THE TINY CORPSE AND PEPPER

FOR a minute or two she stood looking at the house, shivering violently, fighting against the enormous and mindless hunger that kept growing inside her, and wondering what to do next, when suddenly a footman in livery came running out of the wood—(she considered him to be a footman because he was in livery: otherwise, judging by his face only, she would have called him a corpse)—and rapped loudly at the door with his torn and bony knuckles. It was opened by another footman in livery, with a round face, and large eyes; and both footmen, Alice noticed, looked pale and not quite alive, and not quite dead either. They both also smelled terrible; she could smell them even from her distant bush. Each of them also wore strange jeweled collars around their necks. And both had powdered hair that curled all over their heads. She felt very curious to know what it was all about, and crept a little way out of the wood to listen.

The arriving Footman gave a snarling grunt and began by producing from under his arm a great letter, nearly as large as himself, stained by dark blood stains and other unthinkable fluids, and this he handed over to the other, saying, in a solemn tone, "For the Duchess. An Invitation from the Queen to play croquet." The door Footman repeated, in the same solemn tone, only changing the order of the words a little, "From the Queen. An invitation for the Duchess to play croquet."

Then they both bowed low, and their curls got entangled together. And then there was a great tumult of flailing arms and gnashing teeth, and the two footmen were attacking one another, tearing at their powdered wigs and blood stained jackets.

Alice laughed so much at this, that she had to run back into the wood for fear of their hearing her; and when she next peeped out, the delivery

Footman was gone, and the other was sitting on the ground near the door, staring stupidly up into the sky, licking its bony, bloody fingers. Alice didn't like to think what had happened to the other footman, but she saw no corpse lying about, only one of those odd jeweled collars lying in the dust.

Alice went timidly up to the door, and knocked.

"There's no sort of use in knocking," said the Footman, still nibbling at his gore-stained fingers, "and that for two reasons. First, because I'm on the same side of the door as you are; secondly, because they're making such a noise inside, no one could possibly hear you." And certainly there was a most extraordinary noise going on within—a constant howling and sneezing, and every now and then a great crash, as if a dish or kettle had been broken to pieces.

"Please, then," said Alice, "how am I to get in?"

"There might be some sense in your knocking," the Footman went on without attending to her, "if we had the door between us. For instance, if you were *inside*, you might knock, and I could let you out, you know." He was looking up into the sky all the time he was speaking, and this Alice thought decidedly uncivil. "But perhaps he can't help it," she said to herself; "his eyes are so *very* nearly at the top of his head. But at any rate he might answer questions.—How am I to get in?" she repeated, aloud.

"I shall sit here," the Footman remarked, "till tomorrow—"

At this moment the door of the house opened, and a large plate came skimming out, straight at the Footman's head: it just grazed his nose, and broke to pieces against one of the trees behind him.

"—or next day, maybe," the Footman continued in the same tone, exactly as if nothing had happened.

"How am I to get in?" asked Alice again, in a louder tone.

"*Are* you to get in at all?" said the Footman. "That's the first question, you know."

It was, no doubt: only Alice did not like to be told so. "It's really dreadful," she muttered to herself, "the way all the creatures argue. It's enough to drive one crazy!"

The Footman seemed to think this a good opportunity for repeating his remark, with variations. "I shall sit here," he said, "on and off, for days and days."

"But what am I to do?" said Alice.

"Anything you like," said the Footman, and began eating his own fingers in great snapping crunches, moaning in ecstasy as he did so.

"Oh, there's no use in talking to him," said Alice desperately: "he's perfectly idiotic! Eating himself all up! What shall be left in a little while and how will he answer the door without his hands?" And she opened the door and went in.

The door led right into a large kitchen, which was full of smoke from one end to the other: the Duchess was sitting on a three-legged stool in the middle, nursing a baby; the cook was leaning over the fire, stirring a large cauldron which seemed to be full of soup.

The kitchen was dimly lit by the small fire under the cooking pot. Shadows danced along the walls, which looked wet and dripped with something thick and dark. Small skeletons hung from pegs along the walls. Some belonged to various animals—frogs, cats, dogs, pigs, and rabbits, mostly. But there were some that had obviously belonged to small children, and those frightened Alice a great deal. What kind of people had she stumbled across that ate small children?

But Alice's hunger was getting the best of her again and she leaned towards the cooking pot. The delicious scent wafted to her and her mouth began to water; she peeked into the pot and saw dismembered legs and arms swimming in the dark red liquid. Despite her hunger, her eyes began to water as she bent over the smoking pot. "There's certainly too much pepper in that soup!" Alice said to herself, as well as she could for sneezing.

There was certainly too much of it in the air. Even the Duchess sneezed occasionally; and as for the baby, it was sneezing and howling alternately without a moment's pause. The only things in the kitchen that did not sneeze were the cook, and a skinny black cat which was sitting on the hearth and grinning from ear to ear. The cat was dark with gray and black stripes alternating along its emaciated body. Its thin rib cage showed clearly along its sides, and its whiskers looked mangled and torn. But for all that it looked near dead; two fearfully bright eyes looked back at her over its ragged paws. She wasn't sure what made her more uncomfortable: its eyes or its alarmingly sinister and toothy grin.

"Please would you tell me," said Alice, a little timidly, for she was not quite sure whether it was good manners for her to speak first, "why your cat grins like that?"

"It's a Cheshire cat," said the Duchess, "and that's why. *Dead!*"

She said the last word with such sudden violence that Alice quite jumped; but she saw in another moment that it was addressed to the baby, and not to her, so she took courage, and went on again: "I didn't know that Cheshire cats always grinned; in fact, I didn't know that cats *could* grin."

"They all can," said the Duchess; "and most of 'em do."

"I don't know of any that do," Alice said very politely, feeling quite pleased to have got into a conversation.

"You don't know much," said the Duchess; "and that's a fact."

Alice did not at all like the tone of this remark, and thought it would be as well to introduce some other subject of conversation. While she was trying to fix on one, the cook took the cauldron of soup off the fire, and at once set to work throwing everything within her reach at the Duchess and the baby—the fire-irons came first; then followed a shower of saucepans, plates, and dishes, and old bones and ragged grave clothes. The Duchess took no notice of them even when they hit her; and the baby was howling so much already, that it was quite impossible to say whether the blows hurt it or not.

"Oh, *please* mind what you're doing!" cried Alice, jumping up and down in an agony of terror. "Oh, there goes his *delicious* nose," as an unusually large saucepan flew close by it, and very nearly carried it off.

"If everybody minded their own business," the Duchess said in a hoarse growl, "the world would go round a deal faster than it does."

"Which would *not* be an advantage," said Alice, who felt very glad to get an opportunity of showing off a little of her knowledge. "Just think of what work it would make with the day and night! You see the earth takes twenty-four hours to turn round on its axis—"

"Talking of axes," said the Duchess, "chop off her head!"

Alice glanced rather anxiously at the cook, to see if she meant to take the hint; but the cook was busily stirring the soup, and seemed not to be listening, so she went on again: "Twenty-four hours, I *think*; or is it twelve? I—"

"Oh, don't bother *me*," said the Duchess; "I never could abide figures!" And with that she began nursing her child again, singing a sort of lullaby to it as she did so, and giving it a violent shake at the end of every line:

> "Speak roughly to your little boy,
> And beat him when he sneezes:
> He only does it to annoy,
> Because he knows it teases."

CHORUS.

(In which the cook and the baby joined):

"Wow! wow! wow!"

While the Duchess sang the second verse of the song, she kept tossing the baby violently up and down, and the poor little thing howled so, that Alice could hardly hear the words:

"I speak severely to my boy,
I beat him when he sneezes;
For he can thoroughly enjoy
The pepper when he pleases!"

CHORUS.

"Wow! wow! wow!"

"Here! you may nurse it a bit, if you like!" the Duchess said to Alice, flinging the baby at her as she spoke. "I must go and get ready to play croquet with the Queen," and she hurried out of the room. The cook threw a frying-pan after her as she went out, but it just missed her.

Alice caught the baby with some difficulty, as

it was a queer-shaped little creature, and held out its arms and legs in all directions, "just like a sweet little meat pie," thought Alice, licking her lips and smacking her mouth. The poor little thing was snorting like a steam-engine when she caught it, and kept doubling itself up and straightening itself out again, so that altogether, for the first minute or two, it was as much as she could do to hold it.

As soon as she had made out the proper way of nursing it (which was to twist it up into a sort of knot, and then keep tight hold of its right ear and left foot, so as to prevent its undoing itself), she carried it out into the open air. "*If* I don't take this child away with me," thought Alice, "they're sure to kill it in a day or two: wouldn't it be murder to leave it behind?" She said the last words out loud, and the little thing grunted in reply (it had left off sneezing by this time). "Don't grunt," said Alice; "that's not at all a proper way of expressing yourself."

Alice gazed down into the wee face, wondering

if anyone would notice if she took a bite of his fat little cheek, just something to nibble. Surely he had plenty of cheek to go round; no one would be the wiser if she had something to fulfill this mind-numbing hunger inside her. But before she could decide which cheek to taste first, the baby grunted again, and Alice looked very anxiously into its face to see what was the matter with it. There could be no doubt that it had a *very* pale cast to it now, and its eyes were rolled to the back of its head; its pink tongue was now blue and cold: altogether Alice did not like the look of the thing at all. "But perhaps it was only holding its breath to keep from sobbing," she thought, and looked into its eyes again, to see if there were any tears.

No, there were no tears. "If you're going to turn into a corpse, my dear," said Alice seriously, "I'll have nothing more to do with you. Mind now!" The poor little thing groaned and squirmed in her arms and they went on for some while in silence.

Alice was just beginning to think to herself,

"Now, what am I to do with this cold thing when I get it home?" when it groaned again, so violently, that she looked down into its face in some alarm. This time there could be *no* mistake about it: it was neither more nor less than a dead baby, and she felt that it would be quite absurd for her to carry it further.

So she set the little creature down, and felt quite relieved to see it crawl away quietly into the wood. "If it had stayed alive for a bit longer," she said to herself, "it would have made a wonderful meal: but it makes rather a handsome corpse, I think." And she began thinking over other children she knew, who might do very well as dinners and lunches, and was just saying to herself, "if one only knew the right way to serve them—" when she was a little startled by seeing the Cheshire Cat sitting on a bough of a tree a few yards off.

The Cat only grinned when it saw Alice. It looked good-natured, she thought: still it had *very* long claws and a great many teeth and its sleek body was midnight black, so she felt that it ought to be treated with respect.

"Cheshire Puss," she began, rather timidly, as she did not at all know whether it would like the name: however, it only grinned a little wider. "Come, it's pleased so far," thought Alice, and she went on. "Would you tell me, please, which way I ought to go from here?"

"That depends a good deal on where you want to get to," said the Cat.

"I don't much care where—" said Alice.

"Then it doesn't matter which way you go," said the Cat.

"—so long as I get *somewhere*," Alice added as an explanation.

"Oh, you're sure to do that," said the Cat, "if you only walk long enough."

Alice felt that this could not be denied, so she tried another question. "What sort of people live about here?"

"In *that* direction," the Cat said, waving its right paw round, "lives a Hatter: and in *that* direction," waving the other paw, "lives a Dead Hare. Visit either you like: they're both zombies."

"But I don't want to go among dead people," Alice remarked.

"Oh, you can't help that," said the Cat: "we're all dead here. I'm dead. You're dead."

"How do you know I'm dead?" said Alice.

"You must be," said the Cat, "or you wouldn't have come here."

Alice didn't think that proved it at all; however, she went on: "And how do you know that you're dead?"

"To begin with," said the Cat, "a living cat eats mice. You grant that?"

"I suppose so," said Alice.

"Well, then," the Cat went on, "you see, I like to eat little girls, not mice. Although a little girl and a mouse are quite the same in my eyes." And with that the Cheshire Cat's eyes grew wider and wider until they were as large as two saucers full of milk and blood.

"Little girls?" said Alice. Suddenly her shivers were for an altogether different reason as the Cat's teeth glistened under the sickly dim sunlight.

"Yes, indeed. Little girls taste oh so delicious after a swift chase in the forest," said the Cat. "Do you play croquet with the Queen to-day?"

"I should like it very much," said Alice, relieved that the conversation had turned away from eating young girls, "but I haven't been invited yet."

"Surely an oversight, I'm certain," said the Cat. "Not to worry. The Red Queen always greets newcomers and visitors to Zombieland. She's quite particular about making sure they know the rules.

"The rules?" said Alice.

"My goodness, yes, indeed, the rules," said the Cat. "Zombieland could not carry on without rules of some sort or another. All those dead things shambling around the countryside looking for fresh meat...no, the Queen is quite right in making rules."

This made Alice curious: how could one person control all the dead things she'd seen?

And as if Alice had spoken her query aloud, the Cat grinned wider and leaned close. "She partly keeps them in line with her zombie army, you know."

"No, I didn't," said Alice. "Thank you for the information." But that seemed hardly to be all the answer. "How does she control her zombie army, if you please?"

"Not if I please," said the Cat. "If you please, indeed."

"Pardon me." Alice gazed back at the Cat in confusion. "I'm not sure ..."

"Who really is?"

"What?"

"Sure," replied the Cat.

Alice shook her head, feeling as if the Cat's grin had gotten inside her head somehow, and had muddled her thoughts beyond control. "Yes, but the zombie army," she tried again.

The Cheshire Cat's eyes widened with glee. "The collars...don't you see?"

Alice brightened up as it all began to make sense to her. "Do you by chance mean those beautiful jeweled collars I've seen hanging around others' necks?"

"Clever, don't you think?" said the Cat.

Alice mulled it over. "I suppose so, if you say," she said. "But isn't it rather dangerous having all those zombies loose with only pretty jewel collars to control them?"

The Cat sat back on its invisible haunches and shook its scraggly head. "Not if she controls them all."

Alice wanted to ask more questions, but the Cat was beginning to vanish altogether—his eyes were turning watery and not all there. "Wait...the game..." She tried to reach for him, but his ears were now gone as well.

"You'll see me there," said the Cat, and vanished.

Alice was not much surprised at this, she was getting so used to queer things happening. While she was looking at the place where it had been, it suddenly appeared again.

"By-the-bye, what became of the baby?" said the Cat. "I'd nearly forgotten to ask."

"It died, I think," Alice quietly said, just as if the Cat had come back in a natural way.

"I thought it would," said the Cat, and vanished again.

Alice waited a little, half expecting to see it again, but it did not appear, and after a minute or two she walked on in the direction in which the Dead Hare was said to live. "I've seen hatters before," she said to herself; "the Hare will be much the most interesting, and perhaps he won't be dead after all—at least not so dead as said the Cat." As she said this, she looked up, and there was the Cat again, sitting on a branch of a tree.

"Did you say died, or lied?" said the Cat.

"I said died," replied Alice; "and I wish you wouldn't keep appearing and vanishing so suddenly: you make one quite giddy."

"All right," said the Cat; and this time it vanished quite slowly, beginning with the end of the tail, and ending with the grin, which remained some time after the rest of it had gone.

"Well! I've often seen a cat without a grin," thought Alice; "but a grin without a cat! It's the most curious thing I ever saw in my life!"

She had not gone much farther before she came in sight of the house of the Dead Hare: she thought it must be the right house, because the chimneys were shaped like ears and the roof was thatched with fur. It was so large a house, that she did not like to go nearer till she had nibbled some more of the left-hand bit of mushroom, and raised herself to about two feet high: even then she walked up towards it rather timidly, saying to herself, "Suppose it should be dead after all! I almost wish I'd gone to see the Hatter instead!"

CHAPTER VII

AN UNDEAD TEA-PARTY

THERE was a table set out under a spanning and skeletal dead tree in front of the dilapidated house, and the Dead Hare and the Hatter were having tea at it: a thin, pale Dormouse, with bare patches all over its little body, was sitting between them, fast asleep, and the other two were using it as a cushion, resting their bony elbows on it, and talking over its head. "Very uncomfortable for the Dormouse," thought Alice; "only, as it's asleep, I suppose it doesn't mind."

The table was a large one, but the three were all crowded together at one corner of it. All across the table were bloody, overflowing dishes, some smeared with dark fluids that looked decayed and dried too long. Gnawed upon bones lay here and there, and on the ground at their feet. And the smell was nauseating, even to Alice, who was trying to be polite and not notice the stink of death that surrounded the tea party. "No room! No room!" they cried out when they saw Alice coming. "There's *plenty* of room!" said Alice indignantly, and she sat down in a large arm-chair at one end of the table.

"Have some wine," the Dead Hare said in an encouraging tone.

Alice looked all round the table, but there was nothing on it but tea and the dirty dishes and gnawed upon bones. She thought a bone with some meat on it would be nice, perhaps would assuage her gnawing hunger. But she would not grab one—unless, of course, it was offered. "I don't see any wine," she remarked.

"There isn't any," said the Dead Hare.

"Then it wasn't very civil of you to offer it," said Alice angrily.

"It wasn't very civil of you to sit down without being invited," said the Dead Hare.

"I didn't know it was *your* table," said Alice; "it's laid for a great many more than three."

"Your hair wants cutting," said the Hatter. He had been looking at Alice for some time with great curiosity, and this was his first speech. His eyes were hollow and dark; several of his teeth were missing, giving him a smile not unlike a snarl. His hands were digging into the table like claws as he leaned closer to Alice. She could smell a cold decay waft from his mouth.

"You should learn not to make personal remarks," Alice said with some severity; "it's very rude."

The Hatter opened his eyes very wide on hearing this; but all he *said* was, "Why is a raven like a writing-desk?"

"Come, we shall have some fun now!" thought Alice. "I'm glad they've begun asking riddles.—I believe I can guess that," she added aloud.

"Do you mean that you think you can find out the answer to it?" said the Dead Hare.

"Exactly so," said Alice.

"Then you should say what you mean," the Dead Hare went on.

"I do," Alice hastily replied; "at least—at least I mean what I say—that's the same thing, you know."

"Not the same thing a bit!" said the Hatter, snarling at her again. A blue tongue snaked inside the dark of his mouth. It made her shiver. "You might just as well say that 'I see what I eat' is the same thing as 'I eat what I see!'"

"You might just as well say," added the Dead Hare, "that 'I like what I get' is the same thing as 'I get what I like!'"

"You might just as well say," added the Dormouse, who seemed to be talking in his sleep, "that 'I breathe when I sleep' is the same thing as 'I sleep when I breathe!'"

"It *is* the same thing with you," said the Hatter, and here the conversation dropped, and the party sat silent for a minute, while Alice thought over all she could remember about ravens and writing-desks, which wasn't much. Just then a murder of crows burst from the tree overhead, shaking down dead leaves, and the noisome birds exploded into the cloudy air, flying off into the distance. She wondered if the Raven she'd encountered a little while before was part of the disappearing birds as they wheeled into the dark clouds above.

The Hatter was the first to break the silence. "What day of the month is it?" he said, turning to Alice: he had taken his watch out of his pocket, and was looking at it uneasily, shaking it every now and then, and holding it to his ear.

Alice considered a little, and then said "The fourth."

"Two days wrong!" sighed the Hatter. "I told you blood wouldn't suit the works!" he added looking angrily at the Dead Hare.

"It was the *best* blood," the Dead Hare meekly replied.

"Yes, but some crumbs must have got in as

well," the Hatter grumbled: "you shouldn't have put it in with the bread-knife."

The Dead Hare took the watch and looked at it gloomily: then he dipped it into his cup of tea, and looked at it again: but he could think of nothing better to say than his first remark, "It was the *best* blood, you know."

Alice had been looking over his shoulder with some curiosity. "What a funny watch!" she remarked. "It tells the day of the month, and doesn't tell what o'clock it is!"

"Why should it?" muttered the Hatter. "Does *your* watch tell you what year it is?"

"Of course not," Alice replied very readily: "but that's because it stays the same year for such a long time together."

"Which is just the case with *mine*," said the Hatter.

Alice felt dreadfully puzzled. The Hatter's remark seemed to have no sort of meaning in it, and yet it was certainly English. "I don't quite understand you," she said, as politely as she could.

"The Dormouse is asleep again," said the Hatter, and he poured a little cold tea upon its nose.

The Dormouse shook its head impatiently, rattling its tiny bones, and said, without opening its eyes, "Of course, of course; just what I was going to remark myself."

"Have you guessed the riddle yet?" the Hatter said, turning to Alice again.

"No, I give it up," Alice replied: "what's the answer?"

"I haven't the slightest idea," said the Hatter.

"Nor I," said the Dead Hare.

Alice sighed wearily. "I think you might do something better with the time," she said, "than waste it in asking riddles that have no answers."

"If you knew Time as well as I do," said the Hatter, "you wouldn't talk about wasting *it*. It's *him*."

"I don't know what you mean," said Alice.

"Of course you don't!" the Hatter said, tossing his head contemptuously. "I dare say you never even spoke to Time!"

"Perhaps not," Alice cautiously replied: "but I know I have to beat time when I learn music."

"Ah! that accounts for it," said the Hatter, leering at her again, his blue tongue licking at his dry, bloody lips. "He won't stand beating. Now, if you only kept on good terms with him, he'd do almost anything you liked with the clock. For instance, suppose it were nine o'clock in the morning, just time to begin lessons: you'd only have to whisper a hint to Time, and round goes the clock in a twinkling! Half-past one, time for dinner!"

("I only wish it was," the Dead Hare said to itself in a whisper.)

"That would be grand, certainly," said Alice thoughtfully: "but then—I shouldn't be hungry for it, you know."

"Not at first, perhaps," said the Hatter: "but you could keep it to half-past one as long as you liked."

"Is that the way *you* manage?" Alice asked.

The Hatter shook his head mournfully. "Not I!" he replied. "We quarreled last March—just before *he* went mad, you know—" (pointing with his tea spoon at the Dead Hare,) "—it was at the great concert given by the Queen of Hearts, and I had to sing:

> 'Twinkle, twinkle, little bat!
> How I wonder what you're at!'

You know the song, perhaps?"

"I've heard something like it," said Alice.

"It goes on, you know," the Hatter continued, "in this way:

> 'Up above the world you fly,
> Like a tea-tray in the sky.
> Twinkle, twinkle—'"

Here the Dormouse shook itself, and began singing in its sleep "Twinkle, twinkle, twinkle, twinkle—" and went on so long that they had to pinch it to make it stop. In doing so, a bit of the little thing fell to the table—his foot, and Alice looked at it hungrily, her hand moving slowly across the dirty table toward it. The Dormouse saw it and snatched it back again, tucking it close to its bony chest, sniffing indignantly at Alice.

"Well, I'd hardly finished the first verse," said the Hatter, "when the Queen jumped up and bawled out, 'He's murdering the time! Off with his head!'"

"How dreadfully savage!" exclaimed Alice.

"And ever since that," the Hatter went on in a mournful tone, "he won't do a thing I ask! It's always six o'clock now."

A bright idea came into Alice's head. "Is that the reason so many tea-things are put out here?" she asked.

"Yes, that's it," said the Hatter with a sigh: "it's always tea-time, and we've no time to wash the things between whiles."

"Then you keep moving round, I suppose?" said Alice.

"Exactly so," said the Hatter: "as the things get used up."

"But what happens when you come to the beginning again?" Alice ventured to ask.

"Suppose we change the subject," the Dead Hare interrupted, yawning. "I'm getting tired of this. I vote the young lady tells us a story."

"I'm afraid I don't know one," said Alice, rather alarmed at the proposal.

"Then the Dormouse shall!" they both cried. "Wake up, Dormouse!" And they pinched it on both sides at once, popping off two small dead chunks of its rib cage, which the Dormouse grabbed hurriedly, all the while watching Alice as it pulled them back to its body.

The Dormouse slowly looked around at them. "I wasn't asleep," he said in a hoarse, feeble voice: "I heard every word you fellows were saying."

"Tell us a story!" said the Dead Hare.

"Yes, please do!" pleaded Alice.

"And be quick about it," added the Hatter, "or you'll be asleep again before it's done."

"Once upon a time there was a young queen who decided that all dead things should obey her every whim," the Dormouse started slowly, eyes already falling back down in preparation for slumber.

"Wake up!" shouted the Dead Hare. "Keep going! This is my favorite story."

The Dormouse jumped in its seat, startled by the Dead Hare's loud voice. "Yes, yes, quite a story it is." And it began to doze again.

"Oh this will never do," said the Hatter. He reached across the table and pinched the little mouse until its whiskers flew up in pain and surprise.

"What did you do that for?" the Dormouse whined.

"The story," they all three said at once.

"Oh, yes…where was I?"

Alice offered helpfully, "The Queen?"

The Dormouse suddenly leaped from its seat

and looked around in terror. "Where is she? Don't let her find me!"

The Hatter was able to get the Dormouse settled once again. "She isn't here. She is, in fact, nowhere to be seen. Now get back to the story."

But the Dormouse was too disturbed to sit still for a moment. It found a half-full tea cup and drained it with shaking paws. When it finished, it smacked its lips and sat back, seemingly calm now. "Once upon a time there was a queen…"

"Yes, you've already said that," Alice said.

The Dormouse gave her a chilly stare and sniffed, turning away. "You really should learn some manners."

"The story!" demanded the Dead Hare, shaking the little Dormouse until his whiskers began to fall off.

"All right, yes, okay," the Dormouse shoved the Dead Hare away. "The Queen built a box to control them all. The end."

Alice looked around at the Hatter and the Dead

Hare to see if they were satisfied with such an abrupt telling, but neither of them seemed to be listening to the little Dormouse any longer; they were busy gathering up its fallen whiskers, tossing them into their tea cups.

"That's it?" Alice said.

The Dormouse smiled happily and finally allowed itself to look at her. "You liked it? Maybe another one?"

"Yes, yes," said the Hatter and the Dead Hare at the same time before Alice could ask the Dormouse to finish the first one to her satisfaction.

"Once upon a time there were three little sisters," the Dormouse began in a great hurry; "and their names were Elsie, Lacie, and Tillie; and they lived at the bottom of a well—"

"What did they live on?" said Alice, who always took a great interest in questions of eating and drinking.

"They lived on treacle," said the Dormouse, after thinking a minute or two.

"They couldn't have done that, you know," Alice gently remarked; "they'd have been ill."

"So they were," said the Dormouse; "*very* ill."

Alice tried to fancy to herself what such an extraordinary way of living would be like, but it puzzled her too much, so she went on: "But why did they live at the bottom of a well?"

"Take some more tea," the Dead Hare said to Alice, very earnestly.

"I've had nothing yet," Alice replied in an offended tone, "so I can't take more."

"You mean you can't take *less*," said the Hatter: "it's very easy to take *more* than nothing."

"Nobody asked *your* opinion," said Alice.

"Who's making personal remarks now?" the Hatter asked triumphantly. His eyes rolled around in their dark sockets, like wet pebbles, and he gave a half growl, half snicker.

Alice did not quite know what to say to this: so she helped herself to some tea and one of the gnawed-upon bones (the cup was rather smeared with blood and other fluids, but she could no longer control her hunger), and then turned to the Dormouse, and repeated her question. "Why did they live at the bottom of a well?"

The Dormouse again took a minute or two to think about it, and then said, "It was a treacle-well."

"There's no such thing!" Alice was beginning very angrily, but the Hatter and the Dead Hare went. "Sh! sh!" and the Dormouse sulkily remarked, "If you can't be civil, you'd better finish the story for yourself."

"No, please go on!" Alice said very humbly; "I won't interrupt again. I dare say there may be *one*."

"One, indeed!" said the Dormouse indignantly. However, he consented to go on. "And so these three little sisters—they were learning to draw, you know—"

"What did they draw?" said Alice, quite forgetting her promise.

"Treacle," said the Dormouse, without considering at all this time.

"I want a clean cup," interrupted the Hatter: "let's all move one place on." He tossed a chipped and bloodied cup to the ground.

He moved on as he spoke, and the Dormouse followed him: the Dead Hare moved into the Dormouse's place, and Alice rather unwillingly took the place of the Dead Hare. The Hatter was the only one who got any advantage from the change: and Alice was a good deal worse off than before, as the Dead Hare had just upset the milk-jug into his plate. But it did not hold milk; instead thick dark blood, with chunks of torn flesh swimming in it, clopped to the dirty plate and table. She pushed the plate away with a disgusted grimace.

Alice did not wish to offend the Dormouse again, so she began very cautiously: "But I don't understand. Where did they draw the treacle from?"

"You can draw water out of a water-well," said the Hatter. "So I should think you could draw treacle out of a treacle-well—eh, stupid?"

"But they were *in* the well," Alice said to

the Dormouse, not choosing to notice this last remark.

"Of course they were," said the Dormouse; "—well in."

This answer so confused poor Alice, that she let the Dormouse go on for some time without interrupting it.

As it spoke, its fur was falling in little dry clumps at its feet even as it tried in vain to retrieve the stray pieces and put them back.

"They were learning to draw," the Dormouse went on, yawning and rubbing its eyes, for it was getting very sleepy; "and they drew all manner of things—everything that begins with an M—"

"Why with an M?" said Alice.

"Why not?" said the Dead Hare.

Alice was silent, but her curiosity was getting the best of her again. She wanted to hear the story about the Red Queen and how she controlled the dead. She turned to the Hatter, who seemed of the three the least sleepy, and said, "If you please, could you finish the story about how the Queen came to control the zombies?"

For a moment the Hatter only stared at her with his strangely distant gaze and then he shrugged, sipping in vain at his empty tea cup. "I suppose it would not hurt."

"What?" asked Alice, confused again.

"The story," the Hatter replied. "Nothing that isn't already common knowledge except to newcomers and visitors."

Alice settled in her seat and waited eagerly.

The Hatter found a small bone with some meat still on it and nibbled at it for a moment, then he began. "Some say she came from a world outside of Zombieland, but no one can say for sure, and she certainly isn't going to say. She was a poor serving girl at a local pub who happened to be serving the night the King himself came to stay while he was traveling to a far away land to meet a witch and a wizard about acquiring a labor force from their diminutive populace of workers.

Alice frowned in confusion; she'd never heard of such a place before.

The Hatter continued between nibbles at the raw meat on the bone. "She made herself irresistible to the King and soon they were married. Then one day, our fair land was struck down by some dread disease that caused the dead to rise again and seek out fresh flesh. Before long, the whole land was in turmoil and there were more zombies than living. But the Red Queen had fought long and hard to become the Queen and she wasn't about to let a bit of bad luck get in her way. She kept her scientists working day and night to come up with some way to control the undead. I'm not sure how it all worked, but I do know that soon the Queen had an army of the undead under her control and she was using them to destroy those she could not control. At first, just the undead. But as her powers grew and she became more angry with her world, she began to take it out on both the living and the undead. Now she walks the kingdom with her zombie army and her control box, keeping us all in line with fear. And no one dares to defy her because she can turn her undead army against anyone silly enough to do so. Do you see?"

Alice nodded silently, unsure how much of what the Hatter said was true and how much was just make believe.

The Dormouse had closed its eyes by this time, and was going off into a doze; but, on being pinched by the Hatter, it woke up again with a little shriek, and went on: "—that begins with an M, such as mouse-traps, and the moon, and memory, and muchness—you know you say things are 'much of a muchness'—did you ever see such a thing as a drawing of a muchness?"

"Really, now you ask me," said Alice, very much confused, "I don't think—"

"Then you shouldn't talk," said the Hatter.

This piece of rudeness was more than Alice could bear: she got up in great disgust, and walked off; the Dormouse fell asleep instantly, and neither of the others took the least notice of her going, though she looked back once or twice, half hoping that they would call after her: the last time she saw them, they were trying to put the Dormouse into the teapot, and his arm was dangling at an alarming angle.

"At any rate I'll never go *there* again!" said Alice as she picked her way through the wood. "It's the stupidest and most disgusting tea-party I ever was at in all my life!"

Just as she said this, she noticed that one of the wind-whipped trees had a door leading right into it. "That's very curious!" she thought. "But everything's curious to-day. I think I may as well go in at once."

And in she went.

Once more she found herself in the long hall, and close to the little glass table. "Now, I'll manage better this time," she said to herself, and began by taking the little golden key, and unlocking the door that led into the graveyard. Then she went to work nibbling at the mushroom (she had kept a piece of it in her pocket) till she was about a foot high: then she walked down the little passage: and *then*—she found herself at last in the wonderfully spooky graveyard, among the tilting tombstones and weeds and decayed crosses.

CHAPTER VIII

THE QUEEN'S GRAVEYARD
CROQUET-GROUND

A large gray tomb stood near the entrance of the graveyard. The roses growing on it were twisted, black, and thorny, but there were three gardeners at it, busily painting them red. Each of the gardeners was pale-faced and smelled terrible. And each wore one of those strange jeweled collars she'd seen on other dead men. Alice thought this a very curious thing, and she went nearer to watch them, and just as she came up to them she heard one of them say, "Look out now, Five! Don't go splashing paint over me like that!"

"I couldn't help it," said Five, in a sulky tone. "Seven jogged my elbow."

On which Seven looked up and said, "That's right, Five! Always lay the blame on others!"

"*You'd* better not talk!" said Five. "I heard

the Queen say only yesterday you deserved to be beheaded!"

"What for?" said the one who had spoken first.

"That's none of *your* business, Two!" said Seven.

"Yes, it *is* his business!" said Five, "and I'll tell him—it was for bringing the cook tulip-roots instead of onions."

Seven flung down his brush, and had just begun "Well, of all the unjust things—" when his eye chanced to fall upon Alice, as she stood watching them, and he checked himself suddenly: the others looked round also, and all of them bowed low, their loose collars clinking in unison like small out-of-tune bells.

"Would you tell me," said Alice, a little timidly, "why you are painting those roses?"

Five and Seven said nothing, but looked at Two. Two began in a low voice, "Why the fact is, you see, Miss, this here tomb ought to have been covered with *red* roses, and we put black ones on it by mistake; and if the Queen was to find it out, we should all have our heads cut off, you know. So you see, Miss, we're doing our best, afore she comes, to—" At this moment Five, who had been anxiously looking across the windswept cemetery, called out "The Queen! The Queen!" and the three gardeners instantly threw themselves flat upon their faces. There was a sound of many footsteps, and Alice looked round, eager to see the Queen.

First came ten soldiers carrying clubs; these were all shaped like the three gardeners, oblong and flat, with their hands and feet at the corners: next the ten courtiers; these were ornamented all over with diamonds, and walked two and two, as the soldiers did. And they, too, wore the jeweled collars round their stiff necks. After these came the royal children; there were ten of them, and the little dears came jumping merrily along hand in hand, in couples: they were all ornamented with hearts. Next came the guests, mostly Kings and Queens, and among them Alice recognized the Black Rat: it was talking in a hurried nervous manner, smiling at everything that was said, and went by without noticing her. Then followed the Knave of Hearts, carrying the King's crown on a crimson velvet cushion; and, last of all this grand procession, came *the King and Queen of Hearts*.

The King was a small man, hardly much taller than Alice herself. He tried to carry himself with greater height and dignity than he actually possessed, which made him rather funny to watch as he hurried to keep up with the Red Queen, who was striding along as if on massive elephant legs.

And it was the Red Queen who Alice found most strangely frightening. Even if she had heard no stories about her cruelty and bloody mindedness, Alice still would have found plenty to be scared of. The Red Queen was an older woman, her dark hair shining with great strands of gray, and her face was broad and unfriendly. Two thin lips seemed to be compressed forcefully at her long mouth. Two beady dark eyes looked out upon the world from narrow peepholes of displeasure. And her broad, horse-like nose flared open with each angry inhalation. She looked down upon those smaller than herself with a sure sense of arrogant power. And in the crook of her left arm, she carried a small metal box, clutched closely to her wide bosom. In her other hand she carried a long wooden stick. It was notched and stained dark along the thick head, as if it had been used in the past for some bloody violence.

Alice was rather doubtful whether she ought not to lie down on her face like the three undead gardeners, but she could not remember ever having heard of such a rule at processions; "and besides, what would be the use of a procession," thought she, "if people had all to lie down upon their faces, so that they couldn't see it?" So she stood still where she was, and waited.

When the procession came opposite to Alice, they all stopped and looked at her, and the Queen said severely "Who is this?" She said it to the Knave of Hearts, who only bowed and smiled in reply.

"Idiot!" said the Queen, tossing her head impatiently; and, turning to Alice, she went on, "What's your name, child?"

"My name is Alice, so please your Majesty," said Alice very politely; but she added, to herself, "Why, they're only a bunch of dead cards, after all. I needn't be afraid of them!"

"And who are *these*?" said the Queen, pointing to the three shivering gardeners who were lying round the tomb; for, you see, as they were lying on their faces, and the pattern on their backs was the same as the rest of the pack, she could not tell whether they were gardeners, or soldiers, or courtiers, or three of her own children.

"How should I know?" said Alice, surprised at her own courage. "It's no business of *mine*."

The Queen turned crimson with fury, and, after glaring at her for a moment like a wild beast, screamed "Off with her head! Off—"

"Nonsense!" said Alice, very loudly and decidedly, and the Queen was silent.

The King laid his hand upon her arm, and timidly said "Consider, my dear: she is only a child!"

The Queen turned angrily away from him, and said to the Knave "Turn them over!"

The Knave did so, very carefully, with one foot.

"Get up!" said the Queen, in a shrill, loud voice, and the three gardeners instantly jumped up, and began bowing to the King, the Queen, the royal children, and everybody else.

"Leave off that!" screamed the Queen. "You make me giddy." And then, turning to the black roses she went on, "What *have* you been doing here?"

"May it please your Majesty," said Two, in a very humble tone, going down on one knee as he spoke, "we were trying—"

"I see!" said the Queen, who had meanwhile been examining the roses. "Off with their heads!" and the procession moved on, three of the soldiers remaining behind to execute the unfortunate dead gardeners, who ran to Alice for protection.

"You shan't be beheaded!" said Alice, and she

put them behind a large, weed-covered gravestone that stood near. The three dead soldiers wandered about for a minute or two, moaning and rolling their eyes, looking for them, and then quietly marched off after the others.

"Are their heads off?" shouted the Queen.

"Their heads are gone, if it please your Majesty!" the soldiers groaned in reply.

"That's right!" shouted the Queen. "Can you play croquet?"

The dead soldiers were silent, and looked at Alice, as the question was evidently meant for her.

"Yes!" shouted Alice.

"Come on, then!" roared the Queen, and Alice joined the procession, wondering very much what would happen next.

"It's—it's a very fine day!" said a timid voice at her side.

She was walking by the Black Rat, who was peeping anxiously into her face, gnashing his teeth and twitching his long black tail nervously.

"Very," said Alice: "—where's the Duchess?"

"Hush! Hush!" said the Rat in a low, hurried tone. He looked anxiously over his shoulder as he spoke, and then raised himself upon tiptoe, put his mouth close to her ear, and whispered, "She's under sentence of execution."

"What for?" said Alice.

"Did you say 'What a pity!'?" the Rat asked.

"No, I didn't," said Alice: "I don't think it's at all a pity. I said 'What for?'"

"She boxed the Queen's ears—" the Rat began. Alice gave a little scream of laughter.

"Oh, hush!" the Rat whispered in a frightened tone. "The Queen will hear you! You see, she came rather late, and the Queen said—"

"Get to your places!" shouted the Queen in a voice of thunder, and people began running about in all directions, tumbling up against each other; however, they got settled down in a minute or two, and the game began. Alice thought she had never seen such a curious croquet-ground in her life; it was all ridges and furrows and tombstones; the balls were zombie heads, the mallets made up of severed human limbs and parts of skeletons, and the dead soldiers had to double themselves up and to stand on their hands and feet, to make the arches.

The chief difficulty Alice found at first was in managing her leg mallet: she succeeded in getting it tucked away, comfortably enough, under her arm, but generally, just as she had got it nicely straightened out, and was going to give the gape-mouthed zombie head a blow with its bony ankle, it *would* twist itself round and try to tickle her nose with its decayed toes so that she could not help bursting out laughing: and when she had got it down, and was going to begin again, it was very provoking to find that the zombie head had stuck out its blue tongue and was in the act of crawling away: besides all this, there was generally a ridge or furrow or headstone in the way wherever she wanted to send the head, and, as the doubled-up soldiers were always getting up and walking off to other parts of the ground, Alice soon came to the conclusion that it was a very difficult game indeed. Meanwhile, her hunger, which she thought taken quite care of by the small snack she'd had at that dreadful tea party, was coming on again, and her leg mallet was beginning to look particularly good for a nibble or two. She looked around cautiously, and when she saw no one was watching, she bent down for a bite. But the leg must've known her intentions because it began to kick and writhe in her grip and she had to give up the idea just so she could keep hold of it.

The players all played at once without waiting for turns, quarreling all the while, and fighting for the wailing, tongue-boosting zombie heads; and in a very short time the Queen was in a furious passion, and went stamping about, and shouting "Off with his head!" or "Off with her head!" about once in a minute.

Alice began to feel very uneasy: to be sure, she

had not as yet had any dispute with the Queen, but she knew that it might happen any minute, "and then," thought she, "what would become of me? They're dreadfully fond of beheading people here; the great wonder is, that there's any one left alive!"

Just then one of the dead soldiers began to wail loudly and waved his arms about. One of the other players tried to quiet it down, but before he could the Red Queen was wading through the weeds, shoving aside the other guests, until she reached the disturbance. Without warning, she swung that heavy wooden stick of hers and struck the wailing soldier in the forehead. Blood and brains exploded in a gory shower and the soldier went dead silent and collapsed to the cold dirt.

The terrified player who had been trying to quiet the wailing zombie soldier looked sidewise at the Red Queen, unsure what to do.

But Alice saw the Red Queen had no such hesitancy: she also struck the player in the head and his skull similarly exploded, sending his brains into the air. The stunned player never had time to speak a word in his defense. Alice felt sick to her stomach at such casual violence and turned away to hide her face.

She was looking about for some way of escape, and wondering whether she could get away without being seen, when she noticed a curious appearance in the air: it puzzled her very much at first, but, after watching it a minute or two, she made it out to be a grin, and she said to herself "It's the Cheshire Cat: now I shall have somebody to talk to."

"How are you getting on?" said the Cat, as soon as there was mouth enough for it to speak with.

Alice waited till the eyes appeared, and then nodded. "It's no use speaking to it," she thought, "till its ears have come, or at least one of them." In another minute the whole black furred head appeared, and then Alice put down her twitching leg mallet, and began an account of the game, feeling very glad she had someone to listen to her. The

Cat seemed to think that there was enough of it now in sight, and no more of it appeared.

"I don't think they play at all fairly," Alice began, in rather a complaining tone, "and they all quarrel so dreadfully one can't hear oneself speak—and they don't seem to have any rules in particular; at least, if there are, nobody attends to them—and you've no idea how confusing it is all the things being undead; for instance, there's the arch I've got to go through next walking about at the other end of the ground—and I should have croqueted the Queen's zombie head just now, only it rolled itself away when it saw mine coming!"

"How do you like the Queen?" said the Cat in a low voice.

"Not at all," said Alice. "She's so extremely—" Just then she noticed that the Queen was close behind her, listening: so she went on, "—likely to win, that it's hardly worth while finishing the game."

The Queen smiled and passed on.

"Who *are* you talking to?" said the King, going

up to Alice, and looking at the Cat's black head with great curiosity.

"It's a friend of mine—a Cheshire Cat," said Alice: "allow me to introduce it."

"I don't like the look of it at all," said the King: "however, it may kiss my hand if it likes."

"I'd rather not," the Cat remarked.

"Don't be impertinent," said the King, "and don't look at me like that!" He got behind Alice as he spoke.

"A cat may look at a king," said Alice. "I've read that in some book, but I don't remember where."

"Well, it must be removed," said the King very decidedly, and he called the Queen, who was passing at the moment, "My dear! I wish you would have this cat removed!"

The Queen had only one way of settling all difficulties, great or small. "Off with his head!" she said, without even looking round.

"I'll fetch the executioner myself," said the King eagerly, and he hurried off.

Alice thought she might as well go back, and see how the game was going on, as she heard the Queen's voice in the distance, screaming with passion. She had already heard her sentence three of the players to be executed for having missed their turns, and she did not like the look of things at all, as the game was in such confusion that she never knew whether it was her turn or not. So she went in search of her zombie head, which unfortunately looked a great deal like all the other moaning, rolling heads on the cemetery field of play that she was confused straight away as to which was which.

Finally she did find hers; it was engaged in a fight with another head, which seemed to Alice an excellent opportunity for croqueting one of them with the other: the only difficulty was, that her leg mallet had pulled itself across to the other side of the graveyard, where Alice could see it trying in a helpless sort of way to dig itself back into the ground, using its rotted heel and grasping toes.

By the time she had caught the leg and brought it back, the fight was over, and both the heads were out of sight: "but it doesn't matter much," thought Alice, "as all the arches are gone from this side of the ground." So she tucked it away under her arm, that it might not escape again, and went back for a little more conversation with her friend.

As she passed by one of the dead soldiers, she stopped to admire the strange jeweled collar. It seemed to be welded together rather clumsily, so much so that when she reached up to test it, the thing fell off the soldier's neck and fell to the ground.

Suddenly the soldier began to stumble and moan, his eyes rolling round in his head. His teeth began to gnash terribly and he turned on Alice. She fell back, and the soldier reached for her. But before he could touch her, a small squad of soldiers were advancing on their mate and bearing long sharp axes. A swing, a swipe, and the zombie soldier's head went flying off to join the other heads gnashing and tonguing at the ground around her.

The poor dead soldier's body fell to the ground next to his collar. The other soldiers gazed at the loosed collar in suspicion.

Alice said nothing and hurried away. Oh, how she hoped the Red Queen didn't hear about that.

When she got back to the Cheshire Cat, she was surprised to find quite a large crowd collected round it: there was a dispute going on between the executioner, the King, and the Queen, who were all talking at once, while all the rest were quite silent, and looked very uncomfortable.

The moment Alice appeared, she was appealed to by all three to settle the question, and they repeated their arguments to her, though, as they all spoke at once, she found it very hard indeed to make out exactly what they said.

The executioner's argument was, that you couldn't cut off a head unless there was a body to cut it off from: that he had never had to do such a thing before, and he wasn't going to begin at *his* time of life.

The King's argument was, that anything that had a head could be beheaded, and that you weren't to talk nonsense.

The Queen's argument was, that if something wasn't done about it in less than no time she'd have everybody executed, all round. (It was this last remark that had made the whole party look so grave and anxious.)

Alice could think of nothing else to say but "It belongs to the Duchess: you'd better ask *her* about it."

"She's in prison," the Queen said to the executioner: "fetch her here." And the executioner went off like an arrow.

The Cat's scraggly black head began fading away the moment he was gone, and, by the time he had come back with the Duchess, it had entirely disappeared; so the King and the executioner ran wildly up and down looking for it, while the rest of the party went back to the game.

CHAPTER IX

THE CORPSE TURTLE'S STORY

You can't think how glad I am to see you again, you dear old thing!" said the Duchess, as she tucked her arm affectionately into Alice's, and they walked off together.

Alice was very glad to find her in such a pleasant temper, and thought to herself that perhaps it was only the pepper that had made her so savage when they met in the kitchen.

"When *I'm* a Duchess," she said to herself, (not in a very hopeful tone though), "I won't have any pepper in my kitchen *at all*. Soup does very well without—Maybe it's always pepper that makes people hot-tempered," she went on, very much pleased at having found out a new kind of rule, "and vinegar that makes them sour—and chamomile that makes them bitter—and—and barley-sugar and such things that make children sweet-tempered. I only wish people knew that: then they wouldn't be so stingy about it, you know—"

She had quite forgotten the Duchess by this time, and was a little startled when she heard her voice close to her ear. "You're thinking about something, my dear, and that makes you forget to talk. I can't tell you just now what the moral of that is, but I shall remember it in a bit."

"Perhaps it hasn't one," Alice ventured to remark.

"Tut, tut, child!" said the Duchess. "Everything's got a moral, if only you can find it." And she squeezed herself up closer to Alice's side as she spoke.

Alice did not much like keeping so close to her: first, because the Duchess was *very* ugly; and secondly, because she was exactly the right height to rest her chin upon Alice's shoulder, and it was an uncomfortably sharp chin. However, she did not like to be rude, so she bore it as well as she could.

"The game's going on rather better now," she said, by way of keeping up the conversation a little.

"'Tis so," said the Duchess: "and the moral of that is—'Oh, 'tis love, 'tis love, that makes the world go round!'"

Alice thought perhaps it was a nice juicy meat pie that did the trick instead, but she kept that to herself, for even thinking on a sweet meat pie was making her stomach grumble and roil with hunger. Instead, Alice whispered, "Somebody said that it's done by everybody minding their own business!"

"Ah, well! It means much the same thing," said the Duchess, digging her sharp little chin into Alice's shoulder as she added, "and the moral of *that* is—'Take care of the sense, and the sounds will take care of themselves.'"

"How fond she is of finding morals in things!" Alice thought to herself. "I wonder what moral she would find in me taking a nice big bite of her cheek." And for a moment, Alice seriously contemplated it, for the older woman's powdered, pocked cheek was well within biting range, and Alice's stomach was still demanding meat; but she forced herself to keep her teeth to herself. She wouldn't want to risk hearing yet another moral from the Duchess. She'd heard quite enough as it was.

"I dare say you're wondering why I don't put my arm round your waist," the Duchess said after a pause: "the reason is, that I'm doubtful about the temper of your leg. Shall I try the experiment?"

For a moment, Alice was confused by her remark, but then remembered she still carried her squirming leg mallet under her arm. "*He* might kick," Alice cautiously replied, not feeling at all anxious to have the experiment tried.

"Very true," said the Duchess: "legs and mustard both have a kick. And the moral of that is— 'Birds of a feather flock together.'"

"Only mustard isn't a bird," Alice remarked.

"Right, as usual," said the Duchess: "what a clear way you have of putting things!"

"It's a mineral, I *think*," said Alice.

"Of course it is," said the Duchess, who seemed ready to agree to everything that Alice said; "there's a large mustard-mine near here. And the moral of that is—'The more there is of mine, the less there is of yours.'"

"Oh, I know!" exclaimed Alice, who had not attended to this last remark, "it's a vegetable. It doesn't look like one, but it is."

"I quite agree with you," said the Duchess; "and the moral of that is—'Be what you would seem to be'—or if you'd like it put more simply—'Never imagine yourself not to be otherwise than what it might appear to others that what you were or might have been was not otherwise than what you had been would have appeared to them to be otherwise.'"

"I think I should understand that better," Alice said very politely, "if I had it written down: but I can't quite follow it as you say it." And even the dismembered leg must have been weary of the Duchess because it began to squirm most irritably and Alice had to use both hands to keep it in place.

"That's nothing to what I could say if I chose," the Duchess replied, in a pleased tone.

"Pray don't trouble yourself to say it any longer than that," said Alice.

"Oh, don't talk about trouble!" said the Duchess. "I make you a present of everything I've said as yet."

"A cheap sort of present!" thought Alice. "I'm glad they don't give birthday presents like that!" But she did not venture to say it out loud.

"Thinking again?" the Duchess asked, with another dig of her sharp little chin.

"I've a right to think," said Alice sharply, for her hunger was beginning to become monstrous again, and she felt she must have meat soon or fall down and die.

"Just about as much right," said the Duchess, "as pigs have to fly; and the m—"

But here, to Alice's great surprise, the

Duchess's voice died away, even in the middle of her favorite word "moral," and the arm that was linked into hers began to tremble. Alice looked up, and there stood the Queen in front of them, with her arms folded, frowning like a thunder-storm. Her mouth was dripping with what Alice thought must be fresh blood, as if she had been eating something not altogether cooked. The blood was smeared down her dress front, and Alice was sure she could see bits of it in her di-sheveled hair as well.

"A fine day, your Majesty!" the Duchess began in a low, weak voice.

"Now, I give you fair warning," shouted the Queen, stamping on the ground and spitting blood at them as she spoke; "either you or your head must be off, and that in about half no time! Take your choice!"

The Duchess took her choice, and was gone in a moment.

"Let's go on with the game," the Queen said to

Alice; and Alice was too much frightened to say a word, but slowly followed her back to the grave-yard, shoved along by the cold wind coming in from the dark forest beyond. The Queen still carried that curious metal box under one arm and the bloody, notched stick in the other. Alice tried to stay out of range of the killing stick.

The other guests had taken advantage of the Queen's absence, and were resting atop various tombs and headstones: however, the moment they saw her, they hurried back to the game, the Queen merely remarking that a moment's delay would cost them their lives.

All the time they were playing the Queen never left off quarrelling with the other play-ers, and shouting "Off with his head!" or "Off with her head!" Those whom she sentenced were taken into custody by the soldiers, who of course had to leave off being arches to do this, so that by the end of half an hour or so there were no arches left, and all the players, except the King, the Queen, and Alice, were in custody and under sentence of execution.

Then the Queen left off, quite out of breath, and said to Alice, "Have you seen the Corpse Turtle yet?"

"No," said Alice. "I don't even know what a Corpse Turtle is."

"It's the thing Corpse Turtle Soup is made from," said the Queen.

"I never saw one, or heard of one," said Alice.

"Come on, then," said the Queen, "and he shall tell you his history,"

As they walked off together, Alice heard the King say in a low voice, to the company generally, "You are all pardoned." "Come, *that's* a good thing!" she said to herself, for she had felt quite unhappy at the number of executions the Queen had ordered.

They very soon came upon a Gryphon, lying fast asleep in the sun. "Up, lazy thing!" said the Queen, "and take this young lady to see the Corpse

Turtle, and to hear his history. I must go back and see after some executions I have ordered"; and she walked off, leaving Alice alone with the Gryphon. Alice did not quite like the look of the creature, but on the whole she thought it would be quite as safe to stay with it as to go after that savage Queen: so she waited.

The Gryphon, who seemed to be mostly made of scraggly feathers and patchy, mangy fur, sat up and rubbed its eyes: then it watched the Queen till she was out of sight: then it chuckled. "What fun!" said the Gryphon, half to itself, half to Alice.

"What *is* the fun?" said Alice.

"Why, *she*," said the Gryphon. "It's all her fancy, that: they never executes nobody, you know.

Alice gave a sigh of relief and said, "Truly?"

The Gryphon sneered nastily and replied, "No. She eats them of course."

"Eats them?" Alice remembered the smeared blood around the old woman's mouth and gulped.

"No use wasting good meat, is there now?"

The Gryphon rustled its dead looking wings and smiled. "Come on!"

"Everybody says 'come on!' here," thought Alice, as she went slowly after it: "I never was so ordered about in all my life, never!"

They had not gone far before they saw the Corpse Turtle in the distance, sitting sad and lonely on a little ledge of rock, and, as they came nearer, Alice could hear him moaning as if his heart would break. He was a rotting hunk of flesh, white and gray, smelling of saltwater, seaweed, and death. His flappers were eaten down to pasty knobs, and bone stuck through the white meat; his teeth hung in his mouth by strings of dead meat; his eyes were dead ovals that rolled round in his knobby head. She pitied him deeply. "What is his sorrow?" she asked the Gryphon, and the Gryphon answered, very nearly in the same words as before, "It's all his fancy, that: he hasn't got no sorrow, you know. Come on!"

So they went up to the Corpse Turtle, who

looked at them with large eyes full of tears, but said nothing.

"This here young lady," said the Gryphon. "She wants for to know your history, she do."

"I'll tell it her," said the Corpse Turtle in a deep, hollow tone. "Sit down, both of you, and don't speak a word till I've finished."

So they sat down, and nobody spoke for some minutes. Alice thought to herself, "I don't see how he can *even* finish, if he doesn't begin." But she waited patiently.

"Once," said the Corpse Turtle at last, with a deep sigh, "I was a live Turtle."

These words were followed by a very long silence, broken only by an occasional exclamation of "Hjckrrh!" from the Gryphon, and the constant heavy moaning of the Corpse Turtle. Alice was very nearly getting up and saying, "Thank you, sir, for your interesting story," but she could not help thinking there *must* be more to come, so she sat still and said nothing. After all, she wanted to know how he had become a Corpse Turtle, how he had died.

"When we were little," the Corpse Turtle went on at last, more calmly, though still groaning a little now and then, "we went to school in the sea. The master was an old Turtle—we used to call him Tortoise—"

"Why did you call him Tortoise, if he wasn't one?" Alice asked. She was exasperated; he seemed more intent on talking about his childhood and not his death.

"We called him Tortoise because he taught us," said the Corpse Turtle angrily: "really you are very dull!"

"You ought to be ashamed of yourself for asking such a simple question," added the Gryphon; and then they both sat silent and looked at poor Alice, who felt ready to sink into the earth. At last the Gryphon said to the Corpse Turtle, "Drive on, old fellow! Don't be all day about it!" and he went on in these words: "Yes, we went to school in the sea, though you mayn't believe it—"

"I never said I didn't!" interrupted Alice.

"You did," said the Corpse Turtle.

"Hold your tongue!" added the Gryphon, before Alice could speak again. The Corpse Turtle went on. "We had the best of educations—in fact, we went to school every day—"

"*I've* been to a day-school, too," said Alice; "you needn't be so proud as all that."

"With extras?" asked the Corpse Turtle a little anxiously.

"Yes," said Alice, "we learned French and music."

"And washing?" said the Corpse Turtle.

"Certainly not!" said Alice indignantly.

"Ah! then yours wasn't a really good school," said the Corpse Turtle in a tone of great relief. "Now at *ours* they had at the end of the bill, 'French, music, *and washing*—extra.'"

"You couldn't have wanted it much," said Alice; "living at the bottom of the sea."

"I couldn't afford to learn it," said the Corpse Turtle with a sigh. "I only took the regular course."

"What was that?" inquired Alice.

"Reeling and Writhing, of course, to begin with," the Corpse Turtle replied; "and then the different branches of Arithmetic—Ambition, Distraction, Uglification, and Derision."

"I never heard of 'Uglification,'" Alice ventured to say. "What is it?"

The Gryphon lifted up both its paws in surprise. "What! Never heard of uglifying!" it exclaimed. "You know what to beautify is, I suppose?"

"Yes," said Alice doubtfully: "it means— to—make—anything—prettier."

"Well, then," the Gryphon went on, "if you don't know what to uglify is, you *are* a simpleton."

Alice did not feel encouraged to ask any more questions about it, so she turned to the Corpse Turtle, and said "What else had you to learn?"

"Well, there was Mystery," the Corpse Turtle replied, counting off the subjects on his flappers, "— Mystery, ancient and modern, with Seaography: then Drawling—the Drawling-master was an old conger-eel, that used to come once a week: *he* taught us Drawling, Stretching, and Fainting in Coils."

"What was *that* like?" said Alice.

"Well, I can't show it you myself," the Corpse Turtle said: "I'm too stiff. And the Gryphon never learnt it."

"Hadn't time," said the Gryphon: "I went to the Classics master, though. He was an old crab, *he* was."

"I never went to him," the Corpse Turtle said with a sigh: "he taught Laughing and Grief, they used to say."

"So he did, so he did," said the Gryphon, sighing in his turn; and both creatures hid their faces in their paws.

"And how many hours a day did you do lessons?" said Alice, in a hurry to change the subject.

"Ten hours the first day," said the Corpse Turtle: "nine the next, and so on."

"What a curious plan!" exclaimed Alice.

"That's the reason they're called lessons," the Gryphon remarked: "because they lessen from day to day."

This was quite a new idea to Alice, and she thought it over a little before she made her next remark. "Then the eleventh day must have been a holiday?"

"Of course it was," said the Corpse Turtle.

"And how did you manage on the twelfth?" Alice went on eagerly.

"That's enough about lessons," the Gryphon interrupted in a very decided tone: "tell her something about the games now."

"But wait," Alice snapped, angry that he refused to get round to the point of the story. "How did you become a Corpse Turtle, if you please?"

The Corpse Turtle groaned again and tried to scuttle its dead body off the rock. It was the Gryphon that answered: "It was the Red Queen, of course. She killed him, used his flippers for soup."

Alice shivered, feeling sickened by the old

woman's cruelty. Why had she not used his whole body for the soup instead of leaving him stuck on a rock with no way to get back to his sea home?

The Corpse Turtle finally gave up, and turned back to Alice and the Gryphon. "No use trying to avoid it. The games it is."

CHAPTER X

THE ZOMBIE LOBSTER QUADRILLE

THE Corpse Turtle sighed deeply, and tried to draw back one ragged stump of a flapper across his dead white eyes. He looked at Alice, and tried to speak, but for a minute or two sobs choked his voice. "Same as if he had a bone in his throat," said the Gryphon: and it set to work shaking him and punching him in the back. At last the Corpse Turtle recovered his voice, and he went on again: "You may not have lived much under the sea—" ("I haven't," said Alice)—"and perhaps you were never even introduced to a lobster—" (Alice began to say "I once tasted—" but checked herself hastily, and said "No, never") "—so you can have no idea what a delightful thing a Zombie Lobster Quadrille is!"

"No, indeed," said Alice. "What sort of a dance is it? How can dead things dance?"

"Why," said the Gryphon, "it's quite simple, really. You first must dig up all your dead (if they haven't already seen fit to raise themselves) and then form into a line along the sea-shore—"

"Two lines!" cried the Corpse Turtle. "Seals, turtles, salmon, and so on; then, when you've cleared all the jelly-fish out of the way—"

"*That* generally takes some time," interrupted the Gryphon.

"—you advance twice—"

"Each with a zombie lobster as a partner!" cried the Gryphon.

"Of course," the Corpse Turtle said: "advance twice, set to partners—"

"—change lobsters, and retire in same order," continued the Gryphon.

"Then, you know," the Corpse Turtle went on, "you throw the—"

"The lobsters!" shouted the Gryphon, with a bound into the air.

"—as far out to sea as you can—"

"Swim after them!" screamed the Gryphon.

"Turn a somersault in the sea!" cried the Corpse Turtle, capering wildly about.

"Change lobsters again!" yelled the Gryphon at the top of its voice.

"Back to land again, and that's all the first figure," said the Corpse Turtle, suddenly dropping his voice; and the two creatures, who had been jumping about like mad things all this time, sat down again very sadly and quietly, and looked at Alice.

"It must be a very pretty dance," said Alice timidly.

"Would you like to see a little of it?" said the Corpse Turtle.

"Very much indeed," said Alice.

"Come, let's try the first figure!" said the Corpse Turtle to the Gryphon. "We can do without lobsters, you know. Which shall sing?"

"Oh, *you* sing," said the Gryphon. "I've forgotten the words."

So they began solemnly dancing round and round Alice, every now and then treading on her toes when they passed too close, small bits of the Corpse Turtle and ratty feathers from the Gryphon falling to the cold sea sand with every new pass, and waving their forepaws to mark the time, while the Corpse Turtle sang this, very slowly and sadly:

"'Will you walk a little faster?' said a
whiting to a snail.
'There's a porpoise close behind us, and
he's treading on my tail.
See how eagerly the lobsters and the turtles
all advance!
They are waiting on the shingle—will you
come and join the dance?
Will you, won't you, will you, won't you,
will you join the dance?
Will you, won't you, will you, won't you,
won't you join the dance?

You can really have no notion how
delightful it will be
When they take us up and throw us, with
the lobsters, out to sea!'
But the snail replied 'Too far, too far!' and
gave a look askance—
Said he thanked the whiting kindly, but he
would not join the dance.
Would not, could not, would not, could not,
would not join the dance.
Would not, could not, would not, could
not, could not join the dance.
'What matters it how far we go?' his scaly
friend replied.
'There is another shore, you know, upon
the other side.
The further off from England the nearer is
to France—
Then turn not pale, beloved snail, but come
and join the dance.
Will you, won't you, will you, won't you,

will you join the dance?
Will you, won't you, will you, won't you,
won't you join the dance?'"

"Thank you, it's a very interesting dance to watch," said Alice, feeling very glad that it was over at last: "and I do so like that curious song about the whiting!"

"Oh, as to the whiting," said the Corpse Turtle, "they—you've seen them, of course?"

"Yes," said Alice, "I've often seen them at dinn—" she checked herself hastily.

"I don't know where Dinn may be," said the Corpse Turtle, "but if you've seen them so often, of course you know what they're like."

"I believe so," Alice replied thoughtfully. "They have their tails in their mouths—and they're all over crumbs."

"You're wrong about the crumbs," said the Corpse Turtle: "crumbs would all wash off in the sea. But they *have* their tails in their mouths; and the reason is—" here the Corpse Turtle yawned and shut his eyes. "Tell her about the reason and all that," he said to the Gryphon.

"The reason is," said the Gryphon, "that they *would* go with the zombie lobsters to the dance. So they got torn apart and thrown out to sea. So they had to fall a long way. So they got their tails fast in their mouths. So they couldn't get them out again. That's all."

"Thank you," said Alice, "it's very interesting. I never knew so much about a whiting before."

"I can tell you more than that, if you like," said the Gryphon. "Do you know why it's called a whiting?"

"I never thought about it," said Alice. "Why?"

"*It does the boots and shoes*," the Gryphon replied very solemnly.

Alice was thoroughly puzzled. "Does the boots and shoes!" she repeated in a wondering tone.

"Why, what are *your* shoes done with?" said the Gryphon. "I mean, what makes them so shiny?"

Alice looked down at them, and considered a little before she gave her answer. "They're done with blacking, I believe."

"Boots and shoes under the sea," the Gryphon went on in a deep voice, "are done with a whiting. Now you know."

"And what are they made of?" Alice asked in a tone of great curiosity.

"Soles and eels, of course," the Gryphon replied rather impatiently: "any shrimp could have told you that."

"If I'd been the whiting," said Alice, whose thoughts were still running on the song, "I'd have said to the porpoise, 'Keep back, please: we don't want *you* with us!'"

"They were obliged to have him with them," the Corpse Turtle said: "no wise fish would go anywhere without a porpoise."

"Wouldn't it really?" said Alice in a tone of great surprise.

"Of course not," said the Corpse Turtle: "why,

if a fish came to *me*, and told me he was going a journey, I should say 'With what porpoise?'"

"Don't you mean 'purpose?'" said Alice.

"I mean what I say," the Corpse Turtle replied in an offended tone. And the Gryphon added "Come, let's hear some of *your* adventures."

"I could tell you my adventures—beginning from this morning," said Alice a little timidly: "but it's no use going back to yesterday, because I was a different person then."

"Explain all that," said the Corpse Turtle.

"No, no! The adventures first," said the Gryphon in an impatient tone: "explanations take such a dreadful time."

So Alice began telling them her adventures from the time when she first saw the Black Rat. She was a little nervous about it just at first, the two creatures got so close to her, one on each side, and opened their eyes and mouths so *very* wide, but she gained courage as she went on. Her listeners were perfectly quiet till she got to the part about her repeating "*You are old, Father William,*" to the Wurm, and the words all coming different, and then the Corpse Turtle drew a long breath, and said "That's very curious."

"It's all about as curious as it can be," said the Gryphon.

"It all came different!" the Corpse Turtle repeated thoughtfully. "I should like to hear her try and repeat something now. Tell her to begin." He looked at the Gryphon as if he thought it had some kind of authority over Alice.

"Stand up and repeat ''*Tis the voice of the sluggard,*'" said the Gryphon.

"How the creatures order one about, and make one repeat lessons!" thought Alice; "I might as well be at school at once." However, she got up, and began to repeat it, but her head was so full of the Zombie Lobster Quadrille, that she hardly knew what she was saying, and the words came very queer indeed:

"'Tis the voice of the Dead Lobster; I heard
him declare,
'You have baked me too brown, I must
sugar my hair.'
As a duck with its eyelids, so he with
his nose
Trims his belt and his buttons, and turns
out his toes.
When the sands are all dry, he is gay as
a lark,
And will talk in contemptuous tones of
the Shark,
But, when the tide rises and sharks
are around,
His voice has a timid and tremulous sound."

"That's different from what I used to say when
I was a child," said the Gryphon.

"Well, I never heard it before," said the Corpse
Turtle; "but it sounds uncommon nonsense."

Alice said nothing; she had sat down with her

face in her hands, wondering if anything would *ever* happen in a natural way again. Her hunger was rising again, and she kept sneaking peeks at the poor Corpse Turtle's pale underbelly, wondering if a piece might fall her way and there was a chance of snatching it up for a snack before the others observed her. All she wanted was a nice place to sit and eat until she didn't feel so dreadfully hungry again.

And why was she so cold now? She had never felt so bone-chillingly cold in her life. Of course, there was the wind off the cold sea; perhaps she hadn't noticed it before. There was an icy look to the red wine waters that made her think of how the blood of a nice rare steak congealed to the bottom of her plate.

And of course all these thoughts of nearly raw, cold meat made her all the more hungry for something like meat pies that she almost wept.

"I should like to have it explained," said the Corpse Turtle, drawing her attention back to her two companions.

"She can't explain it," said the Gryphon hastily. "Go on with the next verse."

"But about his toes?" the Corpse Turtle persisted. "How *could* he turn them out with his nose, you know?"

"It's the first position in dancing," Alice said; but was dreadfully puzzled by the whole thing, and longed to change the subject—perhaps to where she could find some delicious meat pies.

"Go on with the next verse," the Gryphon repeated impatiently: "it begins 'I passed by his garden.'"

Alice did not dare to disobey, though she felt sure it would all come wrong, and she went on in a trembling voice:

> "I passed by his garden, and marked, with one eye,
> How the Owl and the Panther were sharing a pie—
> The Panther took pie-crust, and gravy, and meat,

While the Owl had the dish as its share of
the treat.
When the pie was all finished, the Owl, as
a boon,
Was kindly permitted to pocket the spoon:
While the Panther received knife and fork
with a growl,
And concluded the banquet—"

"What *is* the use of repeating all that stuff," the
Corpse Turtle interrupted, "if you don't explain it
as you go on? It's by far the most confusing thing
I ever heard!"

"Yes, I think you'd better leave off," said the
Gryphon: and Alice was only too glad to do so.
Speaking of meat pies was just too much to bear
in her state of mind. Another tiny bit of the Corpse
Turtle slipped from his dead flappers and she
heard her stomach rumble at the thought of chew-
ing on the succulent cold meat of her companion.

"Shall we try another figure of the Zombie

Lobster Quadrille?" the Gryphon went on. "Or would you like the Corpse Turtle to sing you a song?"

"Oh, a song, please, if the Corpse Turtle would be so kind," Alice replied, so eagerly that the Gryphon said, in a rather offended tone, "Hm! No accounting for tastes! Sing her 'Corpse Turtle Soup,' will you, old fellow?"

The Corpse Turtle sighed deeply, and began, in a voice sometimes choked with sobs, to sing this:

"Beautiful Soup, so rich and green,
Waiting in a hot tureen!
Who for such dainties would not stoop?
Soup of the evening, beautiful Soup!
Soup of the evening, beautiful Soup!
Beau—ootiful Soo—oop!
Beau—ootiful Soo—oop!
Soo—oop of the e—e—evening,
Beautiful, beautiful Soup!

"Beautiful Soup! Who cares for fish,
Game, or any other dish?
Who would not give all else for two
Pennyworth only of beautiful Soup?
Pennyworth only of beautiful Soup?
Beau—ootiful Soo—oop!
Beau—ootiful Soo—oop!
Soo—oop of the e—e—evening,
Beautiful, beauti—FUL SOUP!"

"Chorus again!" cried the Gryphon, and the Corpse Turtle had just begun to repeat it, when a cry of "The trial's beginning!" was heard in the distance.

"Come on!" cried the Gryphon, and, taking Alice by the hand, it hurried off, without waiting for the end of the song.

"What trial is it?" Alice panted as she ran; but the Gryphon only answered "Come on!" and ran the faster, while more and more faintly came, carried on the breeze that followed them, the melancholy words:

"Soo—oop of the e—e—evening,
Beautiful, beautiful Soup!"

CHAPTER XI

WHO STOLE THE MEAT PIES?

THE King and Queen of Hearts were seated on their throne when they arrived, with a great moaning crowd of dead things assembled about them—all sorts of little birds and beasts, as well as the whole pack of cards: the Knave was standing before them, in chains, with a jewel-collared soldier on each side to guard him; and near the King was the Black Rat, with a trumpet in one hand, and a scroll of parchment in the other. In the very middle of the court was a table, with a large dish of steaming meat pies upon it: they looked so good, that it made Alice quite hungry to look at them—"I wish they'd get the trial done," she thought, "and hand round the refreshments!" But there seemed to be no chance of this, so she began looking at everything about her, to pass away the time.

Alice had never been in a court of justice before, but she had read about them in books, and she was quite pleased to find that she knew the name of nearly everything there. "That's the judge," she said to herself, "because of his great wig." The judge, by the way, was the King; and as he wore his crown over the wig, he did not look at all comfortable, and it was certainly not becoming.

But there were some things in this court room that she was sure never were meant to be used in legal proceedings. For one, there were various bodies in various states of decay hanging along the walls, as if to signal the end of all trials. And there were various weapons, from halberds to swords, close to hand where the King and Queen sat.

Near the Red Queen was a small metal box, with bright lights all along its face. The old woman held the box close to her chest, as if protecting it from prying eyes. When she saw Alice looking her way, she turned so the box was hidden by her great bulk.

"Now what could that be?" wondered Alice.

The lights were glittering and reminded her of the strange jeweled collars she saw around the necks of the jurors and most of the soldiers scattered throughout the courtroom. Could it be that the box had something to do with the collars, she wondered. She decided to see if she could get a closer look at the box.

But as she didn't think it possible right now, she turned her attention back to naming the parts of the court room she did recognize.

"And that's the jury-box," thought Alice, "and those twelve zombies," (she was obliged to say "zombies," you see, because all of them were perfectly dead, and in various states of decay; all of them wore those strange jewel collars around their necks, be they beast or bird) "I suppose they are the jurors." She said this last word two or three times over to herself, being rather proud of it: for she thought, and rightly too, that very few little girls of her age knew the meaning of it at all. However, "jury-men" would have done just as well.

Some of the twelve jurors were looking around confused, moaning and drooling; some of them had taken up writing instruments and were writing very busily on slates. A few stabbed themselves in their arms, chests, and cheeks, as if some sort of game. None showed any sign of pain, and after a stab or two, resumed writing again. "What are they doing?" Alice whispered to the Gryphon. "They can't have anything to put down yet, before the trial's begun."

"They're putting down their names," the Gryphon whispered in reply, "for fear they should forget them before the end of the trial."

"Stupid things!" Alice began in a loud, indignant voice, but she stopped hastily, for the Black Rat cried out, "Silence in the court!" and the King put on his spectacles and looked anxiously round, to make out who was talking.

Alice could see, as well as if she were looking over their shoulders, that all the undead jurors were writing down. "Stupid things!" on their slates, and she could even make out that one of them didn't know how to spell "stupid," and that he had to ask his neighbor to tell him. "A nice muddle their slates'll be in before the trial's over!" thought Alice.

One of the zombie jurors had a pencil that squeaked. This of course, Alice could not stand, and she went round the court and got behind him, and very soon found an opportunity of taking it away. She did it so quickly that the poor little dead juror (it was Bill, the Lizard) could not make out at all what had become of it; so, after hunting all about for it, he was obliged to bite the end of one of his little dead fingers and write with the bloody end of it for the rest of the day; and this was of very little use, as it left only smeared, indecipherable marks on the slate.

"Herald, read the accusation!" said the King.

On this the Black Rat blew three blasts on the trumpet, and then unrolled the parchment scroll, and read as follows:

"The Queen of Hearts, she made some
meat pies,
All on a summer day:
The Knave of Hearts, he stole those
meat pies,
And took them quite away!"

"Consider your verdict," the King said to the jury.

"Not yet, not yet!" the Rat hastily interrupted. "There's a great deal to come before that!"

"Call the first witness," said the King; and the Black Rat blew three blasts on the trumpet, and called out, "First witness!"

The first witness was the Hatter. He came in with a teacup in one hand and someone's bloody dismembered hand in the other, of which he was taking little nervous nibbles as he approached. "I beg pardon, your Majesty," he began, "for bringing these in: but I hadn't quite finished my tea when I was sent for."

"You ought to have finished," said the King. "When did you begin?"

The Hatter looked at the Dead Hare, who had followed him into the court, arm-in-arm with the Dormouse. "Fourteenth of March, I think it was," he said.

"Fifteenth," said the Dead Hare.

"Sixteenth," added the Dormouse.

"Write that down," the King said to the jury, and the zombie jury moaned in unison and wrote down all three dates on their slates, and then added them up, and reduced the answer to shillings and pence. Bill the Lizard was too busy nibbling at his own dead fingers to write any more. But since he seemed quiet and happy, no one seemed to mind enough to stop him from devouring himself instead of doing his duty as juror.

"Take off your hat," the King said to the Hatter.

"It isn't mine," said the Hatter.

"Stolen!" the King exclaimed, turning to the jury, who instantly made a memorandum of the fact.

"I keep them to sell," the Hatter added as an explanation; "I've none of my own. I'm a hatter."

Here the Queen put on her spectacles, and began staring at the Hatter, who turned pale and fidgeted. She clutched the metal box close to her chest and sneered.

"Give your evidence," said the King; "and don't be nervous, or I'll have you executed on the spot."

This did not seem to encourage the witness at all: he kept shifting from one foot to the other, looking uneasily at the Queen and that metal box, and in his confusion he bit a large piece out of his teacup instead of the dismembered hand.

Just at this moment Alice felt a very curious sensation, which puzzled her a good deal until she made out what it was: she was beginning to grow larger again, and she thought at first she would get up and leave the court; but on second thoughts she decided to remain where she was as long as there was room for her.

"I wish you wouldn't squeeze so," said the

Dormouse, who was sitting next to her. "I can hardly breathe."

"I can't help it," said Alice very meekly: "I'm growing."

"You've no right to grow here," said the Dormouse.

"Don't talk nonsense," said Alice more boldly: "you know you're growing too."

"Yes, but I grow at a reasonable pace," said the Dormouse: "not in that ridiculous fashion." And he got up very sulkily and crossed over to the other side of the court.

All this time the Queen had never left off staring at the Hatter, and, just as the Dormouse crossed the court, she said to one of the officers of the court, "Bring me the list of the singers in the last concert!" on which the wretched Hatter trembled so, that he shook both his shoes off.

"Give your evidence," the King repeated angrily, "or I'll have you executed, whether you're nervous or not."

"I'm a poor man, your Majesty," the Hatter began, in a trembling voice, "—and I hadn't begun my tea—not above a week or so—and what with the dismembered hand getting so thin—and the twinkling of the tea—"

"The twinkling of the what?" said the King.

"It began with the tea," the Hatter replied.

"Of course twinkling begins with a T!" said the King sharply. "Do you take me for a dunce? Go on!"

"I'm a poor man," the Hatter went on, "and most things twinkled after that—only the Dead Hare said—"

"I didn't!" the Dead Hare interrupted in a great hurry.

"You did!" said the Hatter.

"I deny it!" said the Dead Hare.

"He denies it," said the King: "leave out that part."

"Well, at any rate, the Dormouse said—" the Hatter went on, looking anxiously round to see if he would deny it too: but the Dormouse denied nothing, being fast asleep.

"After that," continued the Hatter, "I cut some more dismembered hand—"

"But what did the Dormouse say?" one of the jury asked.

"That I can't remember," said the Hatter.

"You *must* remember," remarked the King, "or I'll have you executed."

The miserable Hatter dropped his teacup and half-eaten corpse hand, and went down on one knee. "I'm a poor man, your Majesty," he began.

"You're a very poor speaker," said the King.

Here one of the zombie guinea-pigs seemed to shake off some silent hypnosis, and despite the fact he wore one of those jeweled collars, the little rotting thing made a lunge at the dead hand which the Hatter held, and was immediately suppressed by the officers of the court. The soldiers piled on him, fighting to avoid his tiny snapping teeth. (As that is rather a hard word, I will just explain to you how it was done. They had a large canvas bag, which tied up at the mouth with strings: into this they slipped the guinea-pig, head first, and then sat upon it.)

Alice, for all her size, was still trying to figure out a way to get to that metal box. Her curiosity was becoming almost as powerful as her strange hunger now. She was glad for the sudden confusion and used it to edge closer to where the Queen was sitting.

"If that's all you know about it, you may stand down," continued the King.

"I can't go no lower," said the Hatter: "I'm on the floor, as it is."

"Then you may *sit* down," the King replied.

Here another undead guinea-pig gave a great shudder and made a grab for the Hatter's corpse snack, and was suppressed in much the same way by the soldiers. Alice wondered why no one thought it strange that supposedly contrite creatures were suddenly turning violent—and in such a crowded place, too. It seemed to her someone would send out orders to clear the room if such things continued.

But since there didn't seem to be anymore guinea-pigs about, she thought: "Come, that finished the guinea-pigs! Now we shall get on better."

"I'd rather finish my tea," said the Hatter, with an anxious look at the Queen, who was reading the list of singers.

"You may go," said the King, and the Hatter hurriedly left the court, without even waiting to put his shoes on.

"—and just take his head off outside," the Queen added to one of the officers: but the Hatter was out of sight before the officer could get to the door.

Alice was getting close enough to the Queen that she could almost see what the metal box really was…just a few more feet.

"Call the next witness!" said the King.

The next witness was the Duchess's cook. She carried the pepper-box in her hand, and Alice guessed who it was, even before she got into the court, by the way the people near the door began sneezing all at once.

"Give your evidence," said the King.

"Shan't," said the cook.

The King looked anxiously at the Black Rat, who said in a low voice, "Your Majesty must cross-examine *this* witness."

"Well, if I must, I must," the King said, with a melancholy air, and, after folding his arms and frowning at the cook till his eyes were nearly out of sight, he said in a deep voice, "What are tarts made of?"

"Pepper, mostly," said the cook.

"Treacle," said a sleepy voice behind her.

"Collar that Dormouse," the Queen shrieked out. "Behead that Dormouse! Turn that Dormouse out of court! Suppress him! Pinch him! Off with his whiskers!"

For some minutes the whole court was in confusion, getting the Dormouse turned out, and, by the time they had settled down again, the cook had disappeared.

"Never mind!" said the King, with an air of

great relief. "Call the next witness." And he added in an undertone to the Queen, "Really, my dear, *you* must cross-examine the next witness. It quite makes my forehead ache!"

Alice watched the Black Rat as he fumbled over the list, feeling very curious to see what the next witness would be like, "—for they haven't got much evidence *yet*," she said to herself. Imagine her surprise, when the Black Rat read out, at the top of his shrill little voice, the name "Alice!"

CHAPTER XII

ALICE'S RESURRECTION

HERE!" cried Alice, quite forgetting in the flurry of the moment how large she had grown in the last few minutes, and she jumped up in such a hurry that she tipped over the jury-box with the edge of her skirt, upsetting all the zombies on to the heads of the crowd below, and there they lay sprawling about, reminding her very much of a globe of goldfish she had accidentally upset the week before. Some of the undead were making grabs for various members of the frightened and panicked audience. Alice could see one small bird subsumed by three of the zombie jurors and it disappeared in a shower of gore and feathers, with no time for even a squawk. Another zombie juror wrestled with a zombie lobster for a whiting, tearing the poor thing in half with their violent claws.

"Oh, I *beg* your pardon!" she exclaimed in a tone of great dismay, and began picking them up again as quickly as she could, for the accident of the goldfish kept running in her head, and she had a vague sort of idea that they must be collected at once and put back into the jury-box, or they would die.

"The trial cannot proceed," said the King in a very grave voice, "until all the jurymen are back in their proper places—*all*," he repeated with great emphasis, looking hard at Alice as he said do.

The Queen hammered unseen buttons on her metal box and soon the zombies seemed to calm down and stop eating their fellow creatures. She brandished the stick, glowering down into the excited crowd. Her face was enough to quiet them.

Alice looked at the jury-box, and saw that, in her haste, she had put the Lizard in head downwards, and the poor little thing was waving its tail about in a melancholy way, being quite unable to move. To her great dismay, Bill's tail snapped in half and went on wiggling at her feet. She soon got it out again, and put it right; "not that it signifies much," she said to herself; "I should think it would be *quite* as much use in the trial one way up as the other."

As soon as the zombie jury had a little recovered from the shock of being upset, and their slates and pencils had been found and handed back to them, they set to work very diligently to write out a history of the accident, all except the Lizard, who seemed too much overcome to do anything but sit with its mouth open, gazing up into the roof of the court.

"What do you know about this business?" the King said to Alice.

"Nothing," said Alice.

"Nothing *whatever*?" persisted the King.

"Nothing whatever," said Alice.

"That's very important," the King said, turning to the jury. They were just beginning to write this down on their slates, when the Black Rat interrupted: "*Un*important, your Majesty means, of course," he said in a very respectful tone, but frowning and making faces at him as he spoke.

"*Un*important, of course, I meant," the King hastily said, and went on to himself in an undertone, "important—unimportant—unimportant—important—" as if he were trying which word sounded best.

Some of the jury wrote it down "important," and some "unimportant." Alice could see this, as she was near enough to look over their slates; "but it doesn't matter a bit," she thought to herself.

At this moment the King, who had been for some time busily writing in his note-book, cackled out. "Silence!" and read out from his book, "Rule Forty-two. *All persons more than a mile high to leave the court.*"

Everybody looked at Alice.

"*I'm* not a mile high," said Alice.

"You are," said the King.

"Nearly two miles high," added the Queen,

fingering her metal box, eyeing the zombies surrounding her. For the first time, Alice thought the older woman seemed to be a bit frightened by the sheer number of undead that surrounded her and the King. In any case, she clutched tightly at the box for protection. She hefted the killing stick, ready for a moment's use.

"Well, I shan't go, at any rate," said Alice: "besides, that's not a regular rule: you invented it just now."

"It's the oldest rule in the book," said the King.

"Then it ought to be Number One," said Alice.

The King turned pale, and shut his note-book hastily. "Consider your verdict," he said to the jury, in a low, trembling voice.

"There's more evidence to come yet, please your Majesty," said the Black Rat, jumping up in a great hurry; "this paper has just been picked up."

"What's in it?" said the Queen.

"I haven't opened it yet," said the Black Rat, "but it seems to be a letter, written by the prisoner to—to somebody."

"It must have been that," said the King, "unless it was written to nobody, which isn't usual, you know."

"Who is it directed to?" said one of the jurymen.

"It isn't directed at all," said the Black Rat; "in fact, there's nothing written on the *outside*." He unfolded the paper as he spoke, and added "It isn't a letter, after all: it's a set of verses."

"Are they in the prisoner's handwriting?" asked another of they jurymen.

"No, they're not," said the Black Rat, "and that's the queerest thing about it."

"He must have imitated somebody else's hand," said the King.

"Please your Majesty," said the Knave, "I didn't write it, and they can't prove I did: there's no name signed at the end."

"If you didn't sign it," said the King, "that only makes the matter worse. You *must* have meant some mischief, or else you'd have signed your name like an honest man."

There was a general clapping of hands at this: it was the first really clever thing the King had said that day.

"That *proves* his guilt," said the Queen. She was so enraged and red-faced, she quite forgot all about the metal box and let it fall near her feet. Alice took note of it and edged a bit closer to her.

"It proves nothing of the sort!" said Alice. "Why, you don't even know what they're about!"

She could almost touch the box with her foot now.

"Read them," said the King.

The Black Rat put on his spectacles. "Where shall I begin, please your Majesty?" he asked.

"Begin at the beginning," the King said gravely, "and go on till you come to the end: then stop."

These were the verses the Black Rat read:

> "They told me you had been to her,
> And mentioned me to him:
> She gave me a good character,

But said I could not swim.

He sent them word I had not gone
(We know it to be true):
If she should push the matter on,
What would become of you?

I gave her one, they gave him two,
You gave us three or more;
They all returned from him to you,
Though they were mine before.

If I or she should chance to be
Involved in this affair,
He trusts to you to set them free,
Exactly as we were.

My notion was that you had been
(Before she had this fit)
An obstacle that came between
Him, and ourselves, and it.

Don't let him know she liked them best,
For this must ever be
A secret, kept from all the rest,
Between yourself and me."

"That's the most important piece of evidence we've heard yet," said the King, rubbing his hands. "So now let the jury—"

"If any one of them can explain it," said Alice, (she had grown so large in the last few minutes that she wasn't a bit afraid of interrupting him,) "I'll give him sixpence. I don't believe there's an atom of meaning in it." Her big toe was now covering the metal box; the Red Queen seemed to have forgotten all about it as she cowered a bit from Alice.

The zombie jury moaned as one and wrote down on their slates. "*She* doesn't believe there's an atom of meaning in it," but none of them attempted to explain the paper.

"If there's no meaning in it," said the King,

"that saves a world of trouble, you know, as we needn't try to find any. And yet I don't know," he went on, spreading out the verses on his knee, and looking at them with one eye; "I seem to see some meaning in them, after all. '—*said I could not swim*—' you can't swim, can you?" he added, turning to the Knave.

The Knave shook his head sadly. "Do I look like it?" he said. (Which he certainly did *not*, being made entirely of cardboard.)

"All right, so far," said the King, and he went on muttering over the verses to himself: "'*We know it to be true*—' that's the jury, of course—'*I gave her one, they gave him two*—' why, that must be what he did with the meat pies, you know—"

"But, it goes on '*They all returned from him to you*,'" said Alice.

"Why, there they are!" said the King triumphantly, pointing to the meat pies on the table.

"Nothing can be clearer than *that*."

Then again—'*Before she had this fit*—' you

never had fits, my dear, I think?" he said to the Queen.

"Never!" said the Queen furiously, throwing an inkstand at the Lizard as she spoke. (The unfortunate little Bill had left off writing on his slate with one finger, as he found it made no mark; but he now hastily began again, using the ink, that was trickling down his face, as long as it lasted.)

"Then the words don't *fit* you," said the King, looking round the court with a smile. There was a dead silence.

"It's a pun!" the King added in an offended tone, and everybody laughed. "Let the jury consider their verdict," the King said, for about the twentieth time that day.

"No, no!" said the Queen. "Sentence first—verdict afterwards."

"Stuff and nonsense!" said Alice loudly. "The idea of having the sentence first!"

"Hold your tongue!" said the Queen, turning purple.

"I won't!" said Alice.

"Off with her head!" the Queen shouted at the top of her voice. Nobody moved.

"Who cares for you?" said Alice (she had grown to her full size by this time.) "You're nothing but a bunch of dead things!"

And with that, Alice reached down and grabbed the metal box. But with her huge hands, she crushed it without meaning to. The jeweled collars all fell away with a great metallic clatter.

The King and Queen paled and froze. Then the Queen croaked, "Do you know what you've done, you nasty little girl?"

At this the whole room erupted with the hungry moans of zombies, and the undead began to stumble and shamble their way toward the King and Queen. Several of them leaped into the crowd, gnashing teeth and tearing at wailing victims. A small mouse squeaked and was snatched up by a trio of the undead; it was torn apart without so much as a twitch. The zombies moaned in ecstasy and chewed its warm innards, spitting out hunks of bloody fur and bones. Another group of zombies had circled a dodo and were trying to grab it, but the great billed bird was pecking at their rotting hands and seemed to Alice to be coming off with the better of the battle. Bits of the zombies were flying every which way. In the jury-box, two zombies fought over a piece of bloody flesh, clawing at one another in their hungry rage. A large white rabbit tried to dodge a group of the undead, kicking with its wide feet, but the zombies were too intent on their possible meal to feel any discomfort as it knocked bits of them into the jury-box. But finally they closed in on the white rabbit and it didn't stand a chance as they fell upon it with eager groans. The rabbit screamed as its head was ripped from its convulsing body, its feet torn to pieces. Across the room, Alice saw a snarling cat spitting and clawing at the door to the courtroom, trying to escape, as two zombies closed in from either side. It cried out and turned to defend itself.

One zombie lost an eye and the other part of is face to the cat's savage sharp claws. But it did little to slow them down. The cat tried to back away, but the cheekless zombie made a clumsy, but effective, leap for its throat, and before long, the cat was buried under the duo of tearing, biting zombies.

The scene was hellish, as small bands of survivors tried to battle the undead, but ultimately falling to their greater unfeeling numbers.

The Red Queen wasn't going down without a fight, however. She pushed the terrified King before her and kicked him into the gathering dead. The poor little man disappeared under an onslaught of hungry zombies. Alice could hear his screams of agony as they tore him limb from limb.

Meanwhile, the Queen tried to use his death as a distraction and she hurried to back door. But along the way, a zombie who had been hiding behind the judge's bench staggered out in time to catch her long robe. Its dead hands tangled in the fine material and pulled her back. The Queen gave a mighty roar and punched the zombie in the face. Its rotting head collapsed around her huge horny fist and it fell down, releasing her.

Alice could barely see her now, for all the zombies crowding around, but she did see her duck through the back door with a hearty laugh, and then she was gone.

Alice, terrified at what she had done by accident, gave a little scream, half of fright and half of anger. She didn't want to be eaten by these disgusting dead things.

No! No!

Alice swung blindly at the undead as they closed in on her. She felt their tiny teeth sinking into her cool flesh. The smell of death overwhelmed her! She pushed at their heavy weight as they fell upon her.

Her eyes snapped open to a gray sky and dead trees all around.

She found herself lying in the graveyard.

Her sister was shoving her with her foot,

looking down at her crossly. "Wake up, you little brat!"

Alice sat up groggily, brushing away some dead leaves that had fluttered down from the trees upon her face. Her head ached. When she touched where it hurt, she came away with semi-dry blood. Had she hit her head? When had she done that?

She was alive! Not dead, like those things!

She felt her arms and legs and was so happy to be alive she could hardly speak. She touched her hair; none of its came away in her hands; and she could feel all her teeth in her mouth—none had fallen out after all!

"Wake up, Alice!" said her sister. "You dragged me out here so you could sleep for hours!"

"Oh, I've had such a terrible dream!" said Alice, and she told her sister, as well as she could remember them, all these strange Adventures of hers that you have just been reading about, sobbing and shaking; and when she had finished, her sister sneered at her, and said. "Serves you right for hanging around graveyards like a creepy spider." Her sister began to turn away. "Let's go! It's cold out here and I want a meat pie and a nice cup of tea."

So Alice got up and ran off, thinking while she ran, as well she might, what a dreadful nightmare it had been, but already tasting the meat pie. She was so hungry! She would devour two, at least!

Her sister watched her run away with that nasty sneer still on her thin, cruel lips.

Alice and her stupid dreams.

How she hated the little brat! She had come along to ruin a good thing. Everything had been perfectly fine without a baby sister in her life. Now Mother and Father doted on the little brat and treated her second rate.

She sat thinking of Alice and her silly nightmare Adventures, till she too began dreaming after a fashion.

Yes, the meat pie would be especially delicious and satisfying this afternoon, because—

The long grass rustled at her feet as a great Black Rat hurried by.

She snapped out a foot and stomped the nasty little thing until it was dead.

Yes, the meat pies would be wonderful to-day.

She wondered how long it would be before Alice, sweet, stupid little Alice, began to search for her kitten.

She left the graveyard, chuckling to herself.

After she disappeared in the distance, the cold wind moaned through the tombstones and weeds, whispered through the grass where the dead rat lay in a gory pool of its smashed innards and cooling blood. And after a moment, its whiskers began to twitch and quiver with renewed life. Its feet convulsed, scraping at the icy earth, digging little angry furrows and kicking dead leaves all around.

The Black Rat's eyes popped open, bright and red with hungry fury.

ABOUT THE AUTHORS

———

LEWIS CARROLL was born in 1832 and wrote many beloved works of fiction throughout his life. Among some of his most notable works are *Alice's Adventures in Wonderland, Through the Looking-Glass and What Alice Found There,* and *The Hunting of the Snark*. He died in 1898.

NICKOLAS COOK lives in the beautiful Southwestern desert with his wife and four Chinese pugs. He is an editor (*The Black Glove Magazine*) and a horror critic and reviewer, with hundreds of articles in print. He is also the author of a couple of dozen published short stories and three novels, *The Black Beast of Algernon Wood* (Dailey Swan Press), *Baleful Eye* (Stonegarden .net Publishing), and *Alice in Zombieland*, as well as a short story collection, *'Round Midnight and Other Tales of Lost Souls* (Damnation Books). To contact the author email Nickolasecook@aol.com or stop by his official website, *The Horror Jazz and Blues Revue*, at http://thehorrorjazzandbluesrevue .blogspot.com.

ABOUT THE
ILLUSTRATORS

SIR JOHN TENNIEL was an English political cartoonist and illustrator in the late nineteenth century, best remembered today for his illustrations to Lewis Carroll's *Alice's Adventures in Wonderland* and *Through the Looking-Glass*. In 1865 he illustrated the first edition of *Alice*, which was shelved because Tenniel objected to the print quality; a new edition, released in December of the same year, became an instant bestseller, securing Tenniel's lasting fame in the process. His illustrations for both books have taken their place among the most famous literary illustrations ever made, and his colored images were used as models for the costumes in Walt Disney's *Alice in Wonderland*.

BRENT CARDILLO received his degree in illustration from Rhode Island School of Design, specializing in pen and ink work. While he started his career with Marvel, Inc., inking comic books, he has spent the past fifteen years as a children's book designer and art director. He has worked with major licensed children's properties, including Disney, Sesame Workshop, and Nickelodeon, designing and developing concepts for books and children's products. He returned to his roots with *Alice in Zombieland*, using traditional pen and ink techniques with the aid of Photoshop (something Sir John and Lewis Carroll never dreamed of).